Main Street Mysteries

Kudzu Sculptures

by
Diane E. Tatum

From Donna McHugh:

> *Kudzu Sculptures* is a story about newspaper reporter named Dorie Hudson who does some sleuthing work to solve a mystery murder. But can she and Ross MacAvoy find the killer before she becomes the next victim?

This book is an absolute page-turning mystery.

From Deborah Maxey:

> I couldn't put it down. Loved reading it. You have a gift for dialogue …It's a page turner. I loved it
> !

From Kathy Kinsey:

> This is an enjoyable, fast-paced mystery. It

kept me on the edge of my seat.

Dedicated to my husband of 41 years, Ken,
my family,
Dan, Becca, & Kellan
Brad, Julie, Ethan, Paul, & Jonathan
my friends,
my readers,
and my students.

"Woe to you, teachers of the law and Pharisees, you hypocrites! You are like whitewashed tombs, which look beautiful on the outside but on the inside are full of the bones of the dead and everything unclean. In the same way, on the outside you appear to people as righteous, but on the inside, you are full of hypocrisy and wickedness."
Matthew 23:27-28 (NIV)

Chapter 1

Moving to Daelin . . .

Daelin, Georgia, is one of those towns where everybody knows everything about everybody else. Built on the side of a mountain, people can look down into other people's windows and patios. It's a wonder the town needed a newspaper. But if they hadn't had a newspaper, Dorie wouldn't have a job.

Dorie Hudson came to Daelin on a summer day, a ten-hour drive from her Midwestern home, fresh from journalism school at Virginia Tech. Would the deep South be the same as home? Dorie drove her azure compact car into the town square past Confederate statues and a tall stand of foliage covering all the trees at the edge of town. It looked like a herd of elephants linked trunk to tail. It made her smile.

Behind the square rose the mountainside, dotted with elaborate Italianate homes, ivory and ebony dominoes waiting for a certain breeze to cause a chain reaction down the slope. She passed the *Daelin Beacon* newspaper office in the Main Street group of shops and offices in front of her townhome complex. The lights were still on, so she pulled into a spot and went in. A bell rang on the glass door as Dorie entered. She saw a man in the editor's office and poked her head in.

"Hey, Mr. Andrews. I just got into town. Thought I'd pay respects to whoever is still here on a Friday evening."

"Glad you're in Daelin. Monday, eight A.M. We're excited to have you here. That cleared desk is yours. Appreciate it now 'cause by Monday it might be interminably cluttered."

They both laughed, and Dorie made her exit for her loaded down car and the townhouse she'd rented, sight unseen.

Dorie pulled into the parking spot labeled "Reserved for 1246" and popped the trunk. Before Dorie she'd fully climbed out of the car, a red-headed woman ran up to the car, grabbed her, and hugged her tightly.

"Your license plate says Virginia! I love Virginia! Were you a Virginia Tech Hokie?"

"Graduated in May." Dorie wiggled out of the lady's grasp. "I'm Dorie Hudson, the new Lifestyle Editor at the *Beacon*."

"Trudy Jakes was the editor before you. She moved out to Atlanta, to better things, I guess." The lady squinted into the lowering sun. "By the way, I'm Hilde Behan."

Dorie laughed. "Good to know, since we already hugged."

She grabbed a box from the trunk, and Hilde grabbed the suitcase.

"I live next door. We're going to be good friends, I reckon. Being the Lifestyle Editor, you'll need to know all the gossip. I'm plugged into the Daelin grapevine.

I'm your best source."

The Daelin grapevine? Oh my! Dorie smiled and took the suitcase from Hilde after opening the door to her townhome. "Thanks so much. I have much to do before I sleep. We'll have coffee soon."

Hilde took the hint and withdrew from Dorie's front door.

Dorie peeked behind the front curtains waiting for Hilde to get her mail from the unit mailbox and go into her townhome before Dorie went to the car for another box of essentials, like the coffee machine. Whom would Hilde tell about meeting her on her grapevine? She seemed nice enough on the outside. She'd better watch what she said around Hilde.

After another trip to the car, she set up the K-cup coffee machine on the counter. Two mugs on the shelf and her coffee singles in her rotator next to the machine, making breakfast essentials handy. If only she had half and half in the fridge. Grocery store run on the horizon. She went about unpacking her sleeping bag, pillow, nightie, and toothbrush. The moving truck would be at her place in the morning with the rest of her things.

When the moving truck arrived promptly at eight AM, Dorie was sitting on the first step drinking her first cup of coffee. She didn't have many things, but what she did have was precious. Her grandmother's armoire. A dresser from her Aunt Sue. A retro blast from 1950s steel table and chairs from Aunt Mindy. The new queen bed she'd purchased on Memorial Day furniture sales. More boxed stuff from college and home.

Sunday morning, Dorie woke up in her own bed, running late before she ever started. She fixed a K-cup of coffee and hurried to get out the door for church. As she came off the stoop, Dorie bumped into a large man holding a cup of coffee as well. Coffee sloshed over his chest.

"Oops! I'm so sorry!" said Dorie.

He drew a handkerchief from his pocket to clean the coffee from his dress shirt and tie. As she attempted to help him, he brushed her hand away. "You've done enough already." He smelled of coffee and the outdoors. "You must be Dorie Hudson. The neighborhood is abuzz."

"How? I literally just got here."

"You met Hilde. I'm Ross MacAvoy." The morning sun shone through his ginger hair and formed patterns in his well-trimmed beard. "I'm right next door at 1248. Hilde's at 1244. She activated the 'Hilde alert system' last night."

"Hilde alert system?"

"She called her grapevine. She thinks you're perfect for her favorite bachelor." He frowned and removed his tie, dripping with coffee. "That'd be me, by the way."

Dorie covered her mouth and felt hot blood rush to her face.

"Where are you rushing off to?"

"I planned to visit First Church." Dorie's heart skipped a beat.

"I gotta change my shirt. If you want, you can ride with me."

Dorie felt a thrill. "Yes, that would be great."

She waited outside his townhome looking at the big green nursery truck with the sign, "MacAvoy's Nursery and Service." The step up into the cab was huge. Not a good day to wear a tight skirt and high heels.

When Ross emerged from 1248, he offered his hand to stabilize her as she climbed up into the cab. The touch of his hand left her breathless.

When Dorie and Ross arrived at the church, he helped her down from the big green nursery truck. A man at the door offered her a program for worship and directed her to the fellowship hall for coffee and doughnuts. Since she hadn't eaten, she picked up a glazed one and was eying a Boston cream.

"Here she is now! You really must meet Dorie."

The voice was Hilde's. She was dragging a man across the fellowship hall. Ross had slipped away in the crowd like a spirit, leaving her to handle Hilde by herself.

"Meet Mayor Goldstein. Not only is he mayor, he's the head deacon of the church. He's even done baptizing and leading in the Lord's Supper."

"Call me Sonny." He gave her the 'glad hand' as she juggled coffee and a doughnut. "So, you'll be reporting on our fair community? Trudy Jakes was a close friend."

Hilde coughed at the comment.

As quickly as they'd come, they disappeared into the crowd.

The organ music began, inviting the stragglers to come for worship. Dorie gulped the hot coffee and ate most of a doughnut before trashing the rest. She hurried to the sanctuary, slipped into a pew next to Ross, and tried to focus on worship. Familiar hymns helped her feel at home in this unfamiliar place.

~

Ross could feel Dorie's presence beside him in the pew. He wasn't proud of abandoning her at the doughnut table, but how could he allow anyone in after the last disaster of a relationship?

The worship was one long attempt to stay focused on anything but her.

"Stand and join hands with your neighbor. Let's sing our fellowship hymn, 'Blest be the Tie that Binds.'" The organ swelled to the tune with the piano following.

Ross looked at Dorie and took her hand. It was small and smooth and felt right in his grasp.

"Peace to you." She smiled with a crinkle of her freckled nose.

"And to you." He smiled and something inside him broke. She was the one. He could hold her hand for as long as they both shall live. But after relationship disaster, one after another, could he dare risk it? How long before he could tell her without frightening her away?

Ross helped Dorie climb into the cab of his truck. "In okay?"

She smiled. "Can I treat you to lunch?"

"Sure, I'd love to go out to lunch … now."

"Can you recommend someplace that you like? I'm new here, remember?"

Dorie touched his arm, causing that thrill to streak up to his shoulder. The way she arched her eyebrows created that ache like he'd never felt it before. Ross could barely reply. "Mimi's is good for brunch. How's that sound? They make killer muffins and amazing coffee."

"Now coffee, I can get behind as long as it doesn't end up all over you. I'd hate to make you change twice in one morning. By the way, sorry about that. If it stains, I'll buy you a new shirt and tie."

Ross shook his head and smiled. "No worries, News Lady. I don't wear a shirt and tie that often to make any kind of deal over it."

Her smile was like rainbows glinting through the sun shining through the windshield. *Wow, I really need to get this under control. Wait to be invited in. Enjoy this moment.*

"You okay?" Dorie touched his arm again. "I think you just passed the restaurant."

"Guess I need some of that coffee after all. I can turn at the next light and go around the block."

After serious coffee, muffins, fried chicken and greens, Ross took Dorie home, next door to his home. And he found himself wishing only that no wall separated them.

Chapter 2
The Kudzu Situation

The alarm went off at five on Monday. Dorie ran fingers through her bobbed auburn hair while looking into the bathroom mirror. Lots of time to get ready to drive into the strip mall in front of the complex. If only she knew which box held her hair dryer and straightener. After a frenzied search, she settled for the self-drying frizzy look, a bagel, and coffee.

Dorie pulled up to the *Beacon*'s offices at 8:01. *Rats, late on the first day.*

At the ringing of the bell on the door, Mr. Andrews's voice called to her from the back of the office. "Nice of you to join us, Hudson. The news waits for no man or woman."

Dorie threw her things on the desk that was empty on Friday, but now held a mountain of paper in her IN box. Grabbing her graduation-gift-new leather portfolio and pen, she hurried to the conference room in the back of the office. Applause greeted her.

Mr. Andrews named off each person around the table.

"Our new Lifestyles Editor, Dorie Hudson, from someplace cold in the Midwest. Talk to her later. Make her feel at home here" Mr. Andrews was all business. "Dorie, you're covering the town council meeting tonight. We go to press on Tuesday evening. Get info on the kudzu situation."

Dorie nodded, scribbling away on her legal pad. Two of her new coworkers were talking in a low whisper.

"Have you heard from Trudy?"

"Not a word. You know, she and the mayor, uh-huh."

"No! Sonny's a good Christian married man."

"Well, he's a man."

Mr. Andrews continued to drone on while she wished she'd grabbed her laptop instead of paper and pen. Ben was playing solitaire on his laptop, Zach had tetris going, and Sharon was texting on her phone. Dorie could have been Googling info for her assignment.

"That's all, newsies. Go write, create, discover, investigate." Mr. Andrews finally dismissed the team back to their own imaginings.

Back at her desk, Dorie Googled 'kudzu.'

"They are climbing, coiling, and trailing perennial vines native to much of eastern Asia, Southeast Asia, and some Pacific islands…. The plant climbs over trees or shrubs and grows so rapidly that it kills them by heavy shading"

The kudzu situation. What is that all about? One of her search results showed a scene like the elephant sculpture she'd seen on the way into town. She started an article about kudzu. She felt kinship with the plant, transplanted from somewhere else.

It was standing room only in the stuffy town council room. Dorie stood in the back, so she could watch the townsfolk and their reactions.

"Let the meeting come to order." Mayor Goldstein was a short, stout man with a disagreeable toupee. "First on the agenda is Ross MacAvoy with a bee in his bonnet again."

"Mayor?" A timid woman raised her hand and cleared her throat loudly.

"What is it, Sue?"

She shrank into herself at his bellow. "We haven't done the minutes nor the financial report."

"We'll waive all that this month."

Ross stood stoically at the podium in the center of the room. Finally, the mayor waved the gavel toward him.

"Ross, what is eating you *this* month? Say your piece."

"That kudzu is getting worse, and it's suffocating the trees along the road into town. Every year, the town has me kill it. Why is this year different, Sonny?"

"It's like throwing good money after bad." The mayor rolled his eyes.

"This isn't about money. We can't replace old growth loblolly pine. The kudzu must be removed before the stand of pines is dead." Ross's face grew redder, matching his hair.

"We all know who gets the money for saving the trees, don't we?"

"I'd do it for free, if you'd let me."

The two men bantered while the town watched, like it was a tennis match.

"Sorry, Ross, the town has already ruled this issue dead. I see no reason to revive it."

The mayor banged his gavel to dismiss Ross from the podium. A buzz went through the crowd. Ross muttered as he went to his seat at the back of the room. Dorie caught his eye. He nodded to her.

Like that, the 'kudzu situation' was forgotten to tackle the big question of buying another golf cart for the town maintenance staff.

Two hours later the town hall discharged its

citizenry. Dorie grabbed her bags and headed for the Java Joint Coffee Shop to tackle the rough draft of her article. After she'd awakened her computer, she ordered a coffee and received a Wi-Fi code. She found a table in a back corner.

"Here ya go, Darlin'." The barista set her double shot mocha in front of her.

After a sip of the life-giving fluid, she googled Ross MacAvoy. Only info about his business popped up.

She took another sip and felt his presence at her left shoulder, so close she could smell his woodsy aftershave.

"Can I help?"

Dorie calmly closed the window on her laptop and felt the heat flaming her face. "Yes. I don't understand the whole kudzu issue."

Ross smiled. "You and most of the town. I'll get a cup and join you."

Dorie watched him walk across the café. His ginger hair curled at his collar. The sleeves of his red plaid shirt were rolled up to his elbows, accentuating his broad shoulders and muscular arms. Jeans and hiking boots completed his clothing. She turned around, so she wouldn't be caught looking. She typed in the questions she had about kudzu. The questions she had about him she did not record.

Ross returned to the table and scooted the chair out. "What can I tell you about kudzu?"

"Why is there a big conflict over kudzu?"

"Andrews gave you this assignment right out the gate, didn't he?" Ross shook his head. "You know, that's a test?"

Dorie nodded and then sipped her coffee to give him time to organize his thoughts.

The barista brought his coffee and stroked his arm as

she turned to go. "Enjoy, Darlin'."

Ross reddened at the attention and mumbled something affirmative. He then cleared his throat and continued. "Kudzu is not native to the United States. The vine creates a beautiful façade, but it kills whatever it covers." Ross paused to drink his coffee.

"Why is the mayor so torn up over destroying a parasitic vine?"

He shrugged. "Every year the town gives me a contract to kill the growth of kudzu. It's just about impossible to kill completely. This year the mayor decided not to attempt it." His face began to redden. "Why is he willing to allow an old stand of Georgia pine to die?"

Dorie typed his answers. "It's going to be okay, right?"

He banged his fist on the table. "It's not okay! The pine trees are suffocating, and I am legally restrained from saving them."

Dorie closed her laptop. "Legally restrained?"

He tossed an official document from his wallet across the table to her.

Dorie considered the document. "Over kudzu? What if I go see what's under the vines tomorrow morning? My story isn't due till three."

Ross finished his coffee. "I'll drive you to the easiest place in. I just can't get close enough to touch the kudzu. If I do, I'll be arrested for violating the order. What time do you need to be at the *Beacon*?"

"I'm investigating my story, so whenever."

Ross stood. "I'll drive you over at seven A.M. Bring a camera. I want to see what's in there."

"It's a date, um, sure, I'll be ready."

The door jangled as he left. She watched his big green nursery truck drive past the café's doors. A solidly built man with the kiss of sun that belied the time he spent outside. Ginger hair with copper whiskers. Passionate, a man of the Lord. Dorie sighed.

"Yeah, I know. He does that for me too." Angela picked up his cup, then hers. "Refill?"

Chapter 3
Looking inside the kudzu . . .

Dorie walked out her front door at seven. Ross was already in front of her townhome, arms crossed, legs crossed, leaning against his nursery truck. Dorie's breath caught in her throat when she saw him.

"'Morning, News Lady." He opened the door for her. "I'm ready to find out what the mayor is hiding. Something's wrong. I'd lay money on it."

Dorie climbed up into the big truck. Ross closed the door fiercely then hurried around the hood to climb inside. They drove out to the stand of pines that looked like elephants.

"Don't you think it looks like sculpture?" Dorie asked.

"Sure. It's gorgeous for a weed that kills." Ross threw the truck in park and turned off the engine. "I have to wait here. You can go in through that area that looks like a curtain."

"Or a waterfall?" Dorie arched her eyebrow in a question.

"Don't be fooled. It's not so pretty underneath, kind of like some people I know in this town."

Dorie nodded and climbed out of the truck. "Give me your cellphone number; I'll send you pictures."

She climbed in over the vines until she slipped behind

the curtain of foliage. It was dark, so Dorie turned on the flashlight on her phone. The trees looked like bones, skeletons bleached white by time. She texted a picture to Ross. She stumbled over the uneven ground, vines, and tree roots.

Ross texted her, "Keep looking."

The foliage grew denser and more difficult to navigate. The smell was damp and rotten, like compost. The rocks were covered in slippery moss. A dangling vine morphed into a snake in Dorie's mind. She shuddered.

Turning to avoid the snake-like vine, she stumbled and fell into the roots. As she tried to get up, she saw it. She was hovering over the decomposing body of a woman. Stifling a scream, Dorie took several more pictures, one of which included the locket she wore with the monogram TJA. She texted Ross, "Call the police." Then she broke down and cried.

The sirens began immediately. Ross stumbled through the vines and reached out to comfort Dorie as she wept. As the police arrived, Ross slipped the keys to the truck to her.

After observing the scene, they handcuffed and arrested Ross for being in violation of the order to stay away from the kudzu.

"You know the mayor is up to his eyeballs in this. This is Trudy."

The car in the kudzu also seemed to be Trudy's.

The police asked Dorie questions. She asked some of her own. "Who could this be? Who's missing? Who do you suspect?"

"We'll need your clothes since they are covered with remains of our victim."

Lt. Riley McDonough handed her a set of standard issue police department sweats, and she changed, standing on the shaded side of the truck. Her best jeans, too.

Lt. McDonough placed her clothing into an evidence bag. "Follow us to the station. We may have more questions for you."

Dorie climbed into the truck and checked her watch. Noon.

Arriving at the station, she saw Ross being dragged from the cruiser. Dorie followed Ross into the station, but she was directed to the waiting room. Wearing dull gray Daelin Sheriff sweat clothes, she jangled Ross's keys. Dorie realized how naïve she had been. She really didn't know any of these people, especially Ross.

She heard a man announce, "It's Trudy Jakes. The murderer left her purse at the scene."

Gasps of horror and sobbing were followed by excited chatter.

The mayor arrived in handcuffs with Hilde in his wake. Ross emerged, rubbing his wrists. Dorie ran to him, and Ross hugged her. The time was three o'clock.

On Wednesday, Dorie's report and pictures appeared on the front of the *Beacon*. The mayor was in custody since it was no secret that Trudy Jakes had been his mistress. While glad to have found the victim, Dorie was a little freaked out that it was Trudy, whose job she'd taken.

She answered the phone on her desk and recognized Ross's voice.

"Good job, News Lady. Interested in coffee Saturday morning?"

Dorie smiled. "I can drink coffee anytime."

~

Ross hung up and smiled. So much in common. Coffee for one. Christ for another. A wall between them. A murder investigation. He laughed. Not really a requirement for romance, was it?

He strolled through the greenhouse spraying water on

heat sensitive plants. Dorie made him think of how much he'd compromised after his grandfather's death. He had waited for his dream job offer after UGA with the National Forest Service, but the letter never came. So he settled in Daelin, safe and stable. What had that got him? A greenhouse full of trees, bushes, and plants. And a lovely neighbor. Maybe.

"Hey, Ross. I'm looking for some help with rose bush aphids." Hilde startled him from behind. "Got anything for that?"

"Sure, Hilde." He walked over to the pesticides, read some labels, and handed her a spray. "This should do it. Where do you have roses?"

"Oh, not for me, for the mayor. There's no room for anything to grow on our patios at the townhouses!" Hilde handed the spray to Ross to ring up. "How much do I owe you?"

Ross carried it to the cash register and rang it up. "$12."

Hilde handed him a twenty. "Business good?"

"So-so." Ross handed her change and bagged the spray.

"You seem pretty cozy with our new neighbor. She's a cutie, but way too quick on the front page of the *Beacon*, don't cha think?" Hilde leaned on the counter. "Is she too much or what?"

"Dorie's okay. We get along well." Ross handed her the bag. "Since when does being the mayor's secretary make you responsible for the mayor's roses? Shouldn't that be Gina's gig?"

Hilde giggled. "I choose to take care of Sonny the best way I can. Today it's his roses."

"Tomorrow?"

"Maybe something else I can spray. What do you think?"

"Why?" Ross could not understand the allure of

Sonny Goldstein. "Is there no one else you can care about?"

Hilde snorted. "Silly, man." She grabbed the bag and left.

Ross shook his head. What else would Hilde do to get the attention of Sonny Goldstein? Murder?

Chapter 4

Exploring Helen …

Dorie stepped outside her townhouse into a cloud resting on the mountain. Damp and cool for now. Hot and sticky later. Dorie doublechecked the lock on the door and pulled it shut. She saw the curtain move in Hilde's window. *Darn, we're on the Hilde alert system now*. Dorie waved, and the curtain closed.

She skipped off the stoop toward Ross's door.

"You're on time." Ross was leaning against the hood of the green truck. "Unlike many women I've met."

Dorie shook her head. "If I'm ever late, call 911. It's part of my DNA. Dad drilled us in 'on time.' If your behind wasn't in a seat, your behind was left behind."

"I like your dad already. Hop in." He held the door for her and offered his hand for assistance. "'Morning, News Lady. Your chariot awaits."

Ross helped her into the cab of the green monster of a truck. Praising God for stretch jeans, Dorie took his hand and climbed into the cab. In the cup holders were cups from Java Joint. Ross jumped in and started the truck.

"Hey, I thought we were going for coffee, but you've already gone."

Ross nodded. "I want to take you to Helen this morning. I'm sure you haven't had time to go, what with falling into dead bodies and getting accolades for reporting it."

"Why have I heard of Helen, Georgia?" Dorie searched her mind. "Cabbage Patch dolls?"

"Yep. We can go there too if you want. Mocha with a double shot, right?"

Dorie looked at the cups closer and saw her name on one. "Right. How'd you remember?"

He shrugged as he pulled out of the complex onto the road to Helen. "Did you hear they released the mayor on his own recognizance? Said there was only circumstantial evidence concerning Trudy."

Dorie nearly spit her sip of coffee onto his fancy Weather Tech liner. "Seriously? You've got to be kidding."

"Wish I was."

Ross concentrated on the road as it twisted and turned up the mountain. By the time they pulled into the town, Dorie had finished her coffee but was starving. "We are eating, aren't we?"

"Yep." He pulled the truck into the parking lot of Melody's Diner. The lot was packed with cars. "Melody's saving us a booth. I called ahead. It's a popular spot with the locals as well as the tourists."

When Ross walked in, the locals all hallo-ed him. He waved back. A large lady behind the counter pointed to a booth in the back corner. The bacon sizzled, dishes clattered behind the counter, and the coffee splashed in all the cups.

"You've got a girl with you, Ross." She gave a loud whistle, followed by good natured cat-calls.

Dorie waved back, but she could feel the blood rushing into her face, leaving her feeling like a lighthouse of embarrassment. It seemed Ross was quite well-known here. People in Daelin didn't greet Ross when he walked into, well, anywhere as far as she could tell.

"Don't let them bother you. I grew up around here." Ross indicated their booth and stood until she had slid in satisfactorily. "Like Hilde, they all want to see me settled and married. Apparently running your own business successfully doesn't count."

"I think it's the same way everywhere in small town USA." Dorie accepted the menu from the waitress.

"'Morning, Rosso." The waitress handed him the menu. "Don't let this guy get the upper hand, miss. He needs guiding to have a successful relationship. Otherwise, he bolts when it gets too serious."

This time it was Ross who blushed.

"Hi, I'm Emmie, Rosso's first girlfriend all the way back to kindergarten. Dumped me senior year in high school. He came back after college, but he wasn't the same." She clicked open her pen. "Watcha want, Darlin'?"

"Well, it's between breakfast and lunch…"

"Have the mountain breakfast. It has everything on it but the cherry pie." Ross looked over his menu, still blazing red. "Emmie, I'll have the mountain breakfast. Dorie?"

"You had to say cherry pie, didn't you? Is there cherry pie?" Dorie's mouth watered just thinking about it.

"Yes'm there is. You wouldn't be the first this morning to have some neither."

"Yes, then cherry pie, hot chocolate, and a side of hash browns." She grinned. The little girl inside of her was so excited to get pie for breakfast, or whatever this meal was.

"Yes'm, one cherry pie special breakfast coming up." Emmie whisked away their menus and popped off to get their drinks.

"She's cute. Why'd you dump her? She seems nice enough." She knew she'd spoken too soon when Ross's face began to glow again.

"Not much to tell. By the time senior year came about, Emmie started talking about getting married and having a child while I was at UGA. She even tried to get me to … be intimate with her, so she'd get pregnant. That cinched the deal. I didn't need a deceitful woman in my life, for the rest of my life."

"Then I commend you for knowing yourself and for standing up for your values." Dorie could see he was getting stressed. His jaw was moving without sound, and a temple blood vessel throbbed. She reached across the table and took his hand. "It's okay. I know you feel embarrassed, but there's no need."

He let her touch his hand. Then he drew it back when their drinks arrived.

She sipped her hot chocolate. "I'm going to the restroom. I'll be right back."

He nodded, eyes downcast.

~

As Dorie left the table, Emmie slid into her seat. "She's so cute, Ross. Where did you ever come to find her?"

"Emmie, not so loud. She might hear you and run away."

"What, like a fairy in a Shakespearean Midsomer's Night Dream?" She laughed. "I'm sure she's flesh and blood, my lord."

Ross rubbed the back of his neck. "Stop it. I'm trying to make a good impression here. I brought her here to meet you all."

Emmie smiled. "She's lovely, as far as I can tell. 'Course anyone who orders cherry pie before lunch is my kind of girl."

Ross grinned. "She's pretty amazing, isn't she?"

Emmie slid out of the booth and hugged Ross. "You deserve amazing, Ross. I'll go and check on her, so she doesn't escape into the clouds."

~

When Dorie exited the restroom, Ross was still at the table with no food. She slipped out the front door, bell jangling, into the mountain fog, smelling the damp pine trees. Even in fog, she could tell Helen was a special place. The fog wrapped around her like a cool shrug, welcome in summer. She sighed and closed her eyes to appreciate this moment.

The tap on her shoulder startled her back to reality.

"Your food's on the table. Ross was gettin' worried about you. I told him I'd see how you are." It was Emmie, drying her hands on a well-used towel. "He's real special, Miss Dorie. You treat him kind."

Dorie shook her head. "We're just friends. Haven't known each other but a week or so."

"When it's real, you know. I see it in Ross's eyes. Never saw it when it was us." Emmie held the door for Dorie. "He wouldn't have brought you here, among his kith and kin, if it weren't something."

"You think?"

"I know. Just be kind." Emmie threw her arms around Dorie's neck for just a second, then let go. "He's a good man."

Dorie nodded and threaded her way back to the booth.

"Everything okay?" He rose as she entered the area. "I was beginning to worry. Your hot chocolate must be cold."

"It's fine. I just went outside to inhale the fog and the pine."

She noticed his eyes then. Searching hers for any hint of hurt or pain. Caring about her more than she'd seen in any boy's eyes before. Such lovely hazelnut eyes.

He nodded and picked up his fork.

"We could pray over it if you like. My family always

holds hands in restaurants and prays. Unless that makes you uncomfortable."

He smiled then. "I think that's a good idea. Will you say grace?"

Dorie held his hands and prayed over the food and their journey. Once they started eating, the awkwardness abated.

"I wanted to get out of Daelin, so we could talk freely." He sipped his coffee. "I think we can figure out who the murderer is with a little combined brainpower."

"But I don't know anyone!"

"And that's the beauty of it. You don't have preconceived notions about anyone. You see them as they are. I know more than I ever wanted to know. Between the two of us there could be middle ground." Ross finished his omelet and dabbed his lips. "Melody's is always fine."

"The pie and hash browns were great. The hot chocolate needed espresso."

Ross roared with laughter causing the whole restaurant full of diners to turn their direction. "I know a place with an amazing espresso machine. Want to go?"

"Definitely."

Ross scooted back his chair and reached for his wallet.

"I can pay." Dorie reached for her purse.

"Nope. This one's my treat."

Dorie looked into those hazelnut eyes and relented. She'd get the next one.

Chapter 5

Living in Helen, GA …

Ross helped Dorie into the truck. He jumped in and cranked the engine. After a few false starts, it roared to life. He drove to the edge of the lot and made a left onto the state route up into the mountains.

"Where are we going?" Dorie looked behind her to see the road they'd traveled on disappearing in the fog.

"To my home away from home. And I promised you an amazing cup of coffee. I got one of those fancy Ninja Coffee Bars for Christmas." Ross's eyes never left the roadway as it got steeper.

"Wow! Those are nice. Who gave you such a great gift?" Dorie thought it could be from parents or a serious, mysterious girlfriend.

"Technically, I bought it. …I don't have any family left to gift it to me or to buy gifts. Still, it makes a mean cup of Joe."

The truck emerged from the fog like a jetliner flying above the weather. The sun shone brightly, and its heat convinced Dorie to open her window. After a few more minutes, Ross's blinker made Dorie sit up and look around.

"Where are we?"

Ross stopped the truck in front of a ramshackle farm house with a new red, tin roof.

"Home." Ross motioned for her to follow him over to the edge of the yard next to a neglected flower garden. "Take a look at this view. Watch your step. It's a long way down."

Dorie came to him and looked out over the valley. Where the fog had dissipated, she could see Daelin. "It's beautiful. How did you ever come to own such valuable property?"

"Inheritance from my grandparents. My great-grandparents came here from Scotland. They bought it at an estate sale with all their worldly goods. When my grandparents died, this was all they had. It's mine now. I'm rehabbing it."

Dorie followed him to the house. He held the door for her. Ross headed straight for the amazing coffee maker.

"Wow! The granite and cabinets are beautiful. You've done wonderful work here."

Dorie ran her hand along the black granite with silver and blue sparkles in it. The cherry cabinets shone from refinishing. The kitchen floor was trendy ceramic tile.

"Look around while I work magic with the coffee maker."

Dorie wandered through the downstairs. He obviously had done the kitchen first. In the rest of the downstairs, the hardwood floor had been sanded down to the grain, prepared for finishing. The banister and newel post to the second floor had been refinished in the same cherry finish as the kitchen cabinets. The steps were ready to stain as well.

"Can I go upstairs?" When Ross called out his affirmation, she went up the old steps to the bedroom area.

Four large rooms sectioned the top floor. Three were empty and hadn't been touched for many years. The fourth was the master bedroom of a decorator magazine's dream. New carpet, fresh paint, new molding at the floor and the ceiling. A new cherry sleigh bed with matching dresser, night table, and bureau finished off the dreamscape.

Added to the square room was a new master bathroom placed over the garage. A double vanity in marble on cherry cabinetry, marble tile, shower, and separate whirlpool tub completed the perfect master suite, like no old farmhouse had ever seen.

"What do you think?"

Dorie startled. She hadn't heard Ross climb the stairs.

"Perfection. Did you do all of this yourself?"

"I bought the furniture. The coffee's ready."

Dorie followed Ross down the stairs. Coffee mugs sat on a small bistro set in a nook of the kitchen. A yellow legal pad sat between them. Dorie took the seat Ross indicated.

Ross reached for the yellow pad. "Here's a list of everyone I can think of who might have wished to do Trudy harm."

"Before we do that, why are you renting a townhouse in Daelin? You could be living here for nothing." Dorie sipped her coffee while awaiting his answer.

"First, I just finished the master suite this past month, so it wasn't available. Second, my lease runs until the end of the summer. Third, my business is in Daelin. Finally, I have a lovely neighbor I'm just now getting to know. Cheers?" He held up his mug.

Dorie smiled, a warm glow spreading through her that had nothing to do with the coffee. She clinked mugs with him. "Cheers! Who's on your list?"

"Pretty much everyone. Kudzu is not the only thing that covers over ugliness." Ross took a deep sip of his coffee. "What I mean is that Southern sweetness and charm covers a major amount of nastiness in Daelin."

Dorie nodded. "I have experienced this already."

"Exactly. You work at the *Beacon* with Trudy's work

companions. You could sniff out anything strange there. I know her community colleagues and contacts, like the mayor and his staff. You could find out her other sources she'd contact."

"Someone knows something. We'll find out what happened. I'm sure of it."

After their brainstorming session, the yellow pad was full of people to contact. They were full of resolve to see Trudy's murderer brought to justice. A grilled cheese, chips, and soda lunch continued their time in Ross's mountain home.

As the sun lowered in the sky, rays entered the kitchen, signaling time to come down from the mountain and back to everyday life.

As they went to get into the truck, Dorie noticed a generous stand of kudzu enveloping an old truck. "What's happening there?"

"Grandpa's truck. After he died, it was supposed to be mine. By the time I moved back after graduation, the truck was already part of the landscape."

"You never recovered the truck?" Dorie pulled on her seatbelt. "Could it still work?"

Ross shrugged as he started the nursery truck. "It's probably rusted out. I never felt I should move it. Part of this place, y'know. That and too much other work to be done."

Ross fell silent, and Dorie respected his thoughts and memories. When they entered Daelin, Ross pulled the truck into a pizza parlor parking place.

"Pizza?"

"Sounds good."

It was dark and late when Ross and Dorie pulled into the townhouse parking lot in the big green truck. They separated with plans to go to church together the following morning.

Chapter 6

Let the sleuthing begin …

Why does Hilde follow the mayor around like a protective puppy?"

Dorie felt safer asking the question on the way to church, inside Ross's truck, away from sensitive next-door ears.

"Don't know. I never understood why Trudy would prefer Sonny over …" His face flushed, and he turned his attention to the road.

"Over who?" Dorie had unlocked one of Ross's inner closed doors. "Were you and Trudy …?"

Dorie saw Ross struggling with his answer as he made the turn into the church lot. She touched his arm. "You can tell me. I'd never tell something you wanted private."

"Yes, Trudy and I dated for a while. Guess I was too slow to act because before I knew it, she was in that illicit relationship with Sonny. The relationship that got her killed."

"But that makes you one of the suspects, Ross." The words were out of her mouth before she could stop them.

"Perhaps, but I'm the one who cares enough to find her killer."

Ross shifted into park and slammed the door of the truck, leaving Dorie as he stalked into the church. Dorie picked up her Bible and slid the yellow paper out. She pulled a pen from her purse and clicked it open. She added a new column to the page labeled Attachments: Sonny, Ross. Who else had an emotional bond with Trudy?

~

After dropping Dorie off at her townhouse, Ross revved the big truck and headed up the mountain to his true home.

Me? A suspect? What was Dorie thinking? Hadn't they spent enough time together to show her his heart?

Ross downshifted as the transmission groaned at the steepening slope.

They spent all of their free time together. Always on the same frequency. Always amicable and easy. She was everything he wanted. Was he what she wanted?

Ross pulled the truck into the yard. He hopped out about the same time the yard light popped on in the shade of the foliage. Grandpa's truck still mocked him, engulfed in the kudzu vines, undisturbed by time. It greeted him each time he visited his grandparents' home. Eventually he'd tackle the truck, but not today.

He entered the kitchen and hung the keys on the hook by the door. Ross started a cup of coffee and wandered through the house to make sure it was undisturbed. He set his overnight bag at the bottom of the stairs.

Ross stepped out onto the deck with his mug and his Bible. No place to go but to the Lord. *Help me know Dorie and give her safety and intimacy.*

~

Ross's truck was nowhere to be seen Monday morning. Maybe he hid on the mountain after his revelation about his relationship with Trudy. Dorie didn't really think Ross was a suspect, but when starting from scratch, she couldn't assume anything. She was the only one in Daelin who wasn't there when Trudy died.

Dorie made a point of being in the newsroom early on

Monday prior to the morning news meeting. She threw her lunch box into the refrigerator and poured a cup of 'newsroom coffee', one step up from police station coffee. The doughnuts looked tempting, but unnecessary.

"Sharon!" She called out as one of her co-workers arrived. "What's your lunch plan? Want to sit down together today?"

"I didn't have time to make a lunch today." Sharon grabbed two glazed doughnuts. "Or breakfast either."

"Then a bite somewhere? I need to make some friends." Dorie held her breath while Sharon considered her suggestion.

"I usually hang with Marie, you know."

"I'm not exclusive. The three of us could order pizza or something. I just want to get to know you."

"I'll see what Marie wants to do." Sharon stuffed a doughnut in her mouth and poured coffee in her private cup. She nodded to Dorie and waltzed out of the breakroom.

"Gather 'round, Newsies! Time to chart our course for the week." Mr. Andrews called out and rang his brass bell that hung outside the conference room.

Dorie sipped the coffee, grabbed up her tablet from her desk, and headed for the meeting room. How was she going to talk to her colleagues without their 'sniffers' going off?

Marie slid in just as Mr. Andrews started talking, making it impossible to reach out to her about lunch. Sharon wrote a note on Marie's notebook. Marie giggled and looked toward Dorie. She wrote on Sharon's steno pad. They both laughed.

Mean girls who don't let others into their clique. And thick as thieves…. Murderers?

"Hudson, I want you to run with the Trudy murder. You're the only one of us with no preconceived notions about any of us. Do your due diligence, no deadline. Let us know how to help. Everyone will be transparent."

Dorie nodded. The rest of the room went silent and averted their eyes. Great. New girl and designated narc. But permission to dig into Trudy's life.

Once the meeting ended, Dorie headed for the file room to see what Trudy had been working on before her 'move to Atlanta.' She took her yellow list and ticked off each person Trudy had written about, positively with a plus sign, negatively with a minus sign.

~

Ross rolled into Daelin, passing the *Beacon*'s offices. Dorie's blue compact was in the parking lot.

Lord, give her a productive day. Keep her safe. Give me words to speak to encourage her.

The mayor was waiting as Ross pulled into the drive to his nursery. He parked the truck on a side lot and got out to open the gates.

"What's happening, Sonny? It's early on Monday morning for you to pick out new rose bushes or be excited about aphids."

"Not too early to talk to you about your girlfriend interfering in the lives of Daelin citizens. I can tell she is going to be a problem. Do I need to take care of her or can you?"

"Whoa!" Ross unlocked the gate and swung it open. "That sounds like a threat. Does Dorie need to be looking over her shoulder while she does her job? You sound more like a suspect in Trudy's death, or like you're protecting someone else who should be a suspect. Who would that be?"

Sonny walked up to him and poked him in the chest repeatedly. "Now you hear me, MacAvoy. I had nothing to do with Trudy's death. Neither did my wife or my private assistant. Stay away from all of us."

"Still, why did you keep me from destroying the

kudzu. You knew Trudy was in there, didn't you? You sound rather paranoid, mayor. Sure you're not hiding something?" Ross grabbed his hand and thrust it away.

Sonny moved closer to Ross until they were nose to nose. "I'm just saying, stay out of it or else."

Ross took a step back. "Being mayor doesn't make you above the law or give you the right to accost me at my own place of business. And leave Dorie alone. She's not my girlfriend. She's just doing her job. Should I call Riley to arrest and remove you?"

"You wouldn't dare." Sonny snorted and rolled his eyes. "After all, the police answer to me in our small town, y'know? Besides, you and Dorie Hudson are two goody-goodies. You deserve each other."

An involuntary shudder ran up Ross's spine. "We'll see about that." He whipped out his cell phone and dialed 911. Sonny tried to wrestle the phone away from him. Ross struggled with the phone. Sonny slapped him and tried again to take the phone. Ross decked him with a right hook and held the phone up to his ear.

"What is your emergency?"

"Yes, I have someone threatening me with violence in my place of business. Right…at MacAvoy's Nursery,… see someone soon. Thanks."

The sirens started immediately, and the squad car was there just after. Lieutenant McDonough stepped out of his car, gun drawn. Another car arrived just after.

Sonny tried to get up from the ground.

"Just stay put." Lt. McDonough held the gun on the older paunch-bellied man.

Ross shook his hand out. His knuckles were already starting to bruise. "What do women see in him anyway?"

Riley's partner put the cuffs on the mayor and dragged him to the squad car.

"He punched me!" The mayor snorted and puffed. "I'll have you in court, Ross."

"You do that, Sonny. You harassed me on my own land, tried to take my phone, then slapped me. Oh, and also threatened Dorie."

Riley scribbled furiously in his incident book. "Anything else, Ross?"

"He was here before I even arrived with a head full of steam. He intended to threaten me with violence with words and physical intimidation." Ross shook his head. "I have no idea why, but it has to do with the Trudy murder."

Sonny began shouting curse words and threats from the back of the squad car. Ross took his picture. *Right? Good Christian man. What a way to start the week. Dorie can use that when she reports what happened.* Riley's partner slammed the door to the vitriol coming from the backseat.

Ross sent the pic to Dorie. She responded with a thumbs-up emoji.

~

Dorie cried out as Mr. Andrews turned out the light in the file room when he was preparing to leave for the day at seven.

"You been here all day?"

Dorie startled and slid the yellow list into her portfolio. "Guess so, sir. What time is it?"

"Time to go home, Hudson. Points for initiative, but you know you're on salary. No extra pay for missing lunch or staying late." He handed her lunchbox to her. "Go home and eat. Can't catch a murderer on an empty stomach."

"Yes, Mr. Andrews." When she stood, her back screamed from bending over file drawers all day.

"Tomorrow, take the files to your desk." He turned to leave, but returned and hung on the doorframe, filling the only way out of the archives. "And call me Ethan outside the office. Mr. Andrews was my dad."

"Sure." Dorie stretched. "Can I ask you a personal question?" With his nod, she continued. "Did you have a personal relationship with Trudy?"

He shrank back from the doorway just enough for Dorie to sidle past him into the newsroom. Only the red glow from the emergency lighting lit the low cubicle bullpen. He followed her to her desk.

"The simple answer is yes. Not proud of it. It started very simply as friendship. We shared intellectual conversation, and one day we ended up at Chez Jean for lunch. It was the day my wife had her book club event. Didn't know they were meeting at Chez Jean." He laughed. "Never mess with a lady in a wheelchair."

"Wheelchair?"

"Multiple Sclerosis. Can I walk you to your car to make sure you go home safely?"

Dorie breathed a sigh of relief and gathered her notes and computer bag.

Leaving Ethan Andrews in the parking lot, Dorie drove to the Java Joint for coffee and a pastry. Not really dinner or lunch for that matter. She needed to chew on information before real food appeared on her plate.

The bell rang as she stepped into the café.

"Mocha with a double shot of espresso, right?" Angela, the barista, pointed at her for confirmation.

"Absolutely." Dorie was stunned. Yes, she drank a lot of coffee, but had she drunk much of it here?

"Pick a table. I'll bring it to you. Five dollars and seventy-five cents."

Dorie found a table in a back nook, gathered the required fee, then opened her laptop. The Wi-Fi automatically connected. Guess that made her a regular. Her phone buzzed, a new text. Coroner's report to be released and related press conference tomorrow morning. *Could a lady in a wheelchair kill someone then dump the body in the woods?*

"Here ya go. Dorie, right?"

She'd been so engrossed in her thoughts that she startled and nearly knocked the coffee out of the barista's hand.

"Are you okay?" Dorie looked to see if the coffee had spilled.

"I'm good. What about you? Sorry to scare ya like that." She picked up the money and pocketed it in her apron. "Nice job on the piece on Trudy. I hope you find her killer soon. It's hard enough being an independent woman, ya know."

"I do know. Got any chicken salad croissants left?"

"Yeah, I'll bring it to ya, on the house. I still think the mayor's involved."

The picture Ross sent her popped into her mind. "I hear you, Angela." With that. she was gone to find a croissant in the fridge.

Dorie imported the picture from Ross. *I need to see what this was about. Should have asked for chips too.* Dorie sensed a presence before she looked up.

"Thanks. Any chance of getting a bag of chips too?"

"Yeah." The voice was way too deep for Angela. "I thought of those too."

Ross placed the croissant and bag of Baked Ruffles chips next to her and slipped into a seat at her table with his bag of BBQ chips. "Okay if I join you?"

"Thought you were miffed at me." Dorie kept typing while Ross twisted his mouth to come up with a reply.

"You were right. Anyone with connections to Trudy is suspect."

"So, what happened with you and the mayor? Looks like he got arrested in the pic you sent."

"Yep, he threatened and slapped me, so I decked him."

Dorie looked up from her screen. "Why didn't you get arrested?"

"I called 911, he was on my property, and he hit me first."

Dorie rolled her eyes and shook her head. "Boys. Is he still in the clink?"

Ross gave a twisted lip frown. "'Course not. He's the mayor."

"I'll check with Riley for details. Do you think a woman in a wheelchair could murder someone in the woods among the vines and get out without help?"

"Mrs. Andrews?" The barista set Ross's coffee and grilled cheese beside him. "Thanks, Angela."

"You're welcome, Darlin'."

Behind his back, Angela made an interesting sign circling the two of them and hugging herself. Dorie stifled a laugh while Ross turned around in his chair to see what was so funny. Then Angela made a face and headed back to the counter.

"What was that all about?"

Dorie giggled. "It's a girl thing. You wouldn't understand. Yes, Mrs. Andrews. Seems she made quite the scene in a place called Chez Jean because Ethan was out with Trudy."

"Don't know. Depends on cause of death." Ross bit into the toasted cheese sandwich. "Did I hear that the coroner is releasing his report tomorrow?"

"Yep. Everything's about to get interesting." Dorie finally bit into her croissant.

Chapter 7

The mystery deepens …

Tuesday Dorie arrived at the police station just before 8 AM to find most of the town attempting to park in the lot. She drove her blue compact around the block and parked at Java Joint. She waved at Angela who nodded her assent to Dorie's plan. Then she ran to get to the press conference at the police station that was starting at eight.

Standing room was barely attainable. Dorie sidled through the crowd trying to make it to the front. A man grabbed her arm and pulled her to the side of the crowd.

"Get in front of me." Ross stepped aside and allowed her a space in front of him, which put her in front along the side of the overcrowded police lobby.

The *Beacon*'s photographer Justin was kneeling in front, saw her, and shot her a thumb's up. She mouthed 'thank you' to him, especially since she had just realized that her phone was still in the cup holder of her car. He'd get a better picture anyway to accompany her copy for Wednesday's issue.

At 8:05, the police chief entered the lobby, cameras flashed, and the crowd grew frenzied. The chief implored the crowd with hand signals to settle down.

"If y'all let me speak, I'll answer many of your questions. You can receive a copy of the coroner's press release, if you must have it. I will address the particulars in the case. I will not speculate on our suspect list nor on the motive of the crime. We don't know much yet."

A disappointed whisper arose throughout the mob.

"Here's what we do know. The victim found in the stand of kudzu at the edge of town has been positively identified as Trudy Ann Jakes through dental records and various items recovered at the scene. The time of death was approximately June 1 or so when Ms. Jakes had returned to town after her move to Atlanta. The presence of an unidentified drug was found in the remaining stomach contents. That sample has been sent to Atlanta to their crime lab. Despite advanced decomposition, the coroner determined that the cause of death was multiple stab wounds to the abdomen. Ms. Jakes also sustained specific sexual desecration following her death. Ms. Jakes was two months pregnant at the time of the murder."

The sound in the room rose to a crescendo.

"Settle down or I will call us done!" The chief's words had the desired effect as the room quieted immediately.

While everyone in the room was writing frantically or using their smart phones to record the proceedings, Dorie made notes about the people in the room and their reactions to the information being given. Ross whispered in her ear the names of people she did not know yet.

"All I will say about our suspect pool is that it is someone from Daelin. We do not believe trouble followed her from Atlanta. Please remember the family and friends of Trudy in your prayers. We expect no problems in finding our murderer. Don't think you can hide!"

The chief wiped unbidden tears from his face. "That's it. I have no more to say at this time."

Despite the questions being shouted at him, the chief

turned and walked back into the bowels of the station pulling his white handkerchief from a back pocket. Dorie motioned to the photographer. He nodded, yes, he got the shot.

Dorie's mind whirred in all directions. She almost forgot that Ross was standing at her shoulder. When Ross spoke aloud, she jumped.

"Sorry to startle you again. I said, have you had coffee?"

"Actually, I had to park at the Java Joint. I've time for a cup. You?"

He nodded and took her hand as they escaped the mayhem. Riley handed out copies of the coroner's press report at the door. Dorie grabbed one and slipped it into her portfolio with the yellow suspect list. Ross helped her into the green nursery truck and cranked the engine to life.

Dorie went by her car to pick up her phone and laptop. Ross went into the Java Joint to snag a table before the rest of the crowd showed up. The parking lot was filling up quickly as she hurried across to the café, dodging caffeine-deprived adults. The bell jangled as she entered, and Angela pointed to her table in the back where Ross had settled.

"I gave Angela our order. Should be here soon. We beat the rush." Ross jumped up to slide her chair out and slide it back in.

"Pregnant! Who knew she was pregnant? That's motive, Ross." She slid the coroner's press release out and shared it with him.

"Darlin's, good thing you got here when you did. We're gonna run out of your favorite Danish, Ross, so I brought you two. Did you say someone was pregnant?" Angela peered over Ross's shoulder to the coroner's press release. "So, that's why she died." Her normally brash speech dropped away. "Whatever you need, you let me know. You catch the SOB who done this." Angela returned to the counter.

Dorie frowned. "Was it worse that she was pregnant than that she was murdered?"

"News flash, News Lady! You're in the cotton pickin', hell-fire and brimstone, judging, Bible belt South. Being pregnant without marriage is near top of the list. The odd thing is everyone knew the mayor was stepping out with her, even the mayor's wife. People looked the other way. Pregnancy is an outward sign of a private, sinful indiscretion." Ross shook his head. "We are not as enlightened here about such things."

"We need to change our list. Pregnancy changes many things. Who would care that Trudy was pregnant?"

"Mayor Sonny should be at the top of your list. You also might think about your boss Ethan Andrews. That farmer north of town was chasing her too." Angela dropped the plate with a second croissant beside Dorie's coffee. "Figured it wasn't right to treat Ross and withhold from you, Darlin'." Angela hurried back to tend to the line of the coffee-deprived.

Dorie leaned closer to Ross. "She doesn't really like me hanging out here with you, does she?"

"Pay her no mind. Angela hoped to take Emmie's place when we broke up. Angela likes to flirt with the customers. And bring me extra Danish, which I can ill-afford calorie-wise. See, she brought you an extra croissant. She's warming up to you."

"Why aren't you together?" Dorie knew she'd asked the wrong question when Ross's face looked like he was having a coronary. "Not my business. Never mind. Don't answer that."

Ross sputtered a bit. "No, it's not wrong to ask a question to follow up on something I shared but should not have. Fact is, I went to school, and she stayed here, working at Java Joint. We ended up in different places with different goals. She's married to George, who owns the service station. Sometimes I see her at church, alone."

The noise grew exponentially as more people piled into the place. Before they could ask, Angela brought them to-go cups for the coffee and bags for the pastry. She gave them a wink showing a third Danish and croissant in the bag. "I also got you a copy of the *Beacon*. Someone's on front page. See ya later, crime fighters."

Dorie and Ross picked up their to-go vittles and fought their way through the queue to get out the door. Ross walked with Dorie to her car.

Dorie handed him the newspaper. "You keep it for your scrapbook. I'll have one on my desk at work.

Ross put his bag and cup on her car roof. When he opened the paper to the front page, he whistled. "Mayor Goldstein arrested after assault of MacAvoy." He nodded and chuckled.

"So, whatcha think?" Dorie touched his arm. "Did I do you justice?"

"We are so in his sights now." Ross covered her hand with his, just for a second. "I'm talking to Joe this afternoon. I'll let you know how it goes."

Dorie watched as Ross took off with his coffee and Danish for his truck that took up five parking spaces. *What was he thinking? About Trudy? About Sonny? About me?*

Chapter 8

Suspecting others …

Ross pulled the truck up to the barn at Joe's farm north of town. He climbed out of the truck and headed toward the lean man coming out of the house.

"How's it going?" Ross reached out to shake the hand of the farmer.

"Never thought I'd see my seed guy make a house call. What's up, Ross?"

"I wanted to talk about Trudy and you. I know I'm prying, but I'm helping the new reporter at the *Beacon* try to make sense of Trudy's murder."

Ross and Joe sat in the rockers on the porch. No one spoke as Joe picked up his whittling knife and shaved on a piece of white wood.

"What can I tell you?" Joe spit in a cup left for that purpose. "I only went out with her a couple a times."

"Yeah, me too." Ross put a stick of gum in his mouth, trying to be laid back while Joe decided what to tell or not to tell. "Trudy was a fine-looking lady."

"Huh!" Joe spit into the cup for punctuation. "She was carrying on with Sonny. Nothing fine about that."

Ross allowed the silence to persist before continuing. "She didn't think I was the right man for her either. Guess I didn't offer her much."

"I got a hundred acres of fine farm land. Cows. A

sturdy house. And a heart full of love, if she'd wanted it."

Ross willed Joe to tell him what happened. Joe continued to shape whatever it was he was creating. So far it was a pile of white wood shavings.

"I fell in love with her the first time I laid eyes on her. I asked her out. She said yes." He laid the knife down on the table between them. "When I brought her out here for dinner, she seemed happy. So I asked her to marry me on the second date."

"That's pretty sudden, isn't it?" Ross realized he was doing the same with Dorie, though.

"She laughed, told me I was a hick and a fool." Joe stood and leaned against the white porch column. "Laughed. No one should laugh when ya bare your feelings to them."

"That's a shame, Joe." Ross felt the farmer's shame and embarrassment. "Something similar happened to me too. Then she took up with Sonny."

"Still, she needn't have to die." Joe shaded his eyes from the sun. "Gotta have something to do with Sonny."

A pickup truck came barreling down the drive, raising dust behind it. When it stopped, Emmie, from Melody's Diner in Helen, stepped out.

"Hey, Ross. Guess you know my secret now."

Joe smiled and hurried off the porch to greet her. They kissed.

Ross followed him down to the truck. "What secret?"

She held out her left hand. A sparkler of a diamond sat on her ring finger. "Joe and I are getting married. Aren't we, Babe?"

"Yep. Whenever you say and wherever you say." Joe hugged her closer.

"Congrats to you both. I should head back to town."

~

Dorie grabbed the plate of chocolate chip cookies

she'd baked that morning and hopped out of her car. She took a deep breath and climbed the steps onto the expansive columned porch of the mayor's home, one of those Italianate structures on the hill above Daelin proper. The spectacular view looked into the homes of all the residents that fronted the winding road down to Main Street. She rang the bell and waited for the mayor's wife to answer.

"Ms. Hudson, what a surprise." Gina Goldstein swung the door wide. "And with treats. Please do come in."

Dorie entered the tall foyer illuminated by a spectacular chandelier. Gina gestured to a parlor off the foyer where she discovered she was not the only guest of the mayor's wife.

"Hilde." Dorie tried to cover her disappointment. She'd hoped to question Gina alone.

"When do you have time to bake?" Hilde helped herself to one of the cookies as Dorie set them on the coffee table. "You seem to be everywhere. Are you ever home?"

Gina stood with an air of elegance. "I'll just get that pitcher of homemade lemonade I fixed this morning. Make yourself comfortable."

Before Dorie could offer to help, she had whisked away.

Once Gina had left the room, Hilde patted the settee beside her. Dorie joined her.

"Are you suspecting Gina of Trudy's murder?" Hilde took a nibble at the cookie.

Dorie tried to control her blush. "Just trying to get perspective on the citizens of Daelin."

"Oh, I get it. You don't want to let on that she's a suspect."

Gina entered with the promised pitcher of lemonade, making Dorie's intended response inappropriate. Gina poured each of them a tall glass.

Gina took a dainty sip. "So, are you here to ask me tough questions, Ms. Hudson?"

"We can talk another time in private, if you like." Dorie really didn't feel she could speak frankly to Gina with Hilde present.

"I have nothing to hide from Hilde. Ask away." Her words sounded positive, but the tone was cold and challenging.

"How long have you and the mayor been married?" Dorie brought out her notepad. Hilde peeked over her shoulder. Dorie made sure the yellow page was tucked away securely.

"Twenty-five years. No, not always happy years, but wouldn't have done it differently." Gina crossed her legs. "Why don't you ask the question you want to ask?"

"Do you have children?" Dorie hoped she sounded confident, but somehow it felt voyeuristic instead.

"No, we were not able to do so. Does that make me a suspect because Trudy was pregnant?" Gina crossed her arms and tears spilled onto her cheeks. "How do you know if the infertile one was me or Sonny? Why do you assume I would kill over Sonny's indiscretions?"

Hilde crossed the room and wrapped her arms around the mayor's wife. "I think that's enough, Dorie. I know you have a job to do, but you are out of line."

Dorie gathered her things and stood. "I had no desire to offend. I merely wanted to understand."

Gina nodded, a tear streaking down her cheek.

Hilde followed her to the door. "Next time you want to know something about the mayor or his family, ask me. That's part of my job."

Once Dorie was on the front porch, the door slammed soundly. "Interesting."

~

As Dorie entered the *Beacon*'s offices, she heard Mr. Andrews bellow her name. Marie dropped mail on her desk and gave her a rolling-eyes look.

As she passed Sharon's desk, she heard her say, "Now you've done it."

"Yes, Mr. Andrews?" She lightly rapped on the door. "You called for me?"

"Close the door, Hudson."

I am so getting fired. Dorie closed the door and sat in a chair across the desk from the editor. She gripped the arms of the chair, so he couldn't see her shaking.

Mr. Andrews turned his chair around and hung up the phone. In a low growling voice, he said, "I can't believe what you did. No one in this office has ever challenged the mayor or his wife. What were you thinking?"

As she started to stammer, Mr. Andrews waved away her attempt at an explanation.

"Great job. About time someone in this town shook some trees." He grinned. "Find out anything?"

"Nothing that anyone who lives here didn't already know, sir." Dorie wiped her damp palms on her pants. "Would it be okay if I visited your wife?"

"Better yet, come for dinner tonight about six. Bring Ross MacAvoy with you, if you like. I reckon he sold a lot of papers today. Tonight's pizza night. Okay with that?"

Dorie nodded and stood. So much for talking to her alone. "Anything else, sir?"

"Nope. Go write it up."

With that, she left as quickly as she could.

As Dorie passed her, Sharon called out, "Need a box for your things?"

"No thanks. I'm not leaving yet." Dorie caught a glimpse of the glance between Sharon and Marie.

When she returned to her desk, she picked up the yellow envelope Marie had delivered. No postmark or return address. Not a flat letter either. It seemed to rock back and forth. She slit open the edge and looked inside. Then she screamed and dropped it. When it hit the floor, a half-dead rat crawled out.

Leonard, the office clerk, hurried over and efficiently captured the tortured creature in a trash can and disposed of it. Dorie collapsed in her chair.

Jonathan Gates, another *Beacon* reporter, came to her desk and extended his hand. "Congratulations. You are officially a member of the press corps."

Inside the envelope was a ragged, malodorous letter in which the rat had been 'wrapped'. It read, "You don't belong here. Keep your nose out of the Trudy case."

Dorie looked around. Everyone had gone back to work like nothing had happened. Her hands were still shaking when her phone rang. Her screen announced Ross as the caller.

Dorie answered quickly. "Ross, someone sent me a half-dead rat! And we've been invited for pizza at the Andrews's."

"Not sure how to respond to any of that." Ross paused. "Do I need to come and kill the rat? Will it be on the pizza?"

That's when Dorie began to cry and laugh with a tinge of hysteria.

Ross's voice cut through to her. "I'll meet you at the townhomes. Get in your car and drive it into the complex. I'll be there soon."

Dorie tried to stuff down her emotions, but they were out where all could see. She gathered her things and headed for home. Ross was there when she arrived. As she stepped from the car, he gathered her into his arms.

"Let me check your mail and your townhouse for any other threats." Ross turned Dorie toward her front door. "Give me your mail key after you open the front door."

Dorie's hand shook as she inserted the key and turned

it, opening the lock. Then she handed Ross the keys with the mail key upright. He dashed off across the parking lot to the townhomes' central mailboxes. Dorie pushed the door open but waited for Ross to return.

She should have a dog. At least it could kill the rat. Dorie shuddered involuntarily. Who would send her a rat?

"No packages, News Lady. Just bills and a letter from home." Ross handed her the mail and stepped around her. "Let me go in first. It's probably fine, but it doesn't hurt to be cautious."

Dorie nodded and waited to hear his okay. She heard his step on the stairs and his clomping around upstairs. She hoped she hadn't left any intimate items on the floor or hanging on the shower rod.

Ross popped his head out of the door. "Looks okay."

Dorie's hand flew to her mouth, trying to hold in the shriek threatening to escape.

"Hey, girl. It's okay." He reached for her, and she turned into his embrace. "I'm being overly cautious, but it's not everyday someone sends you a live rat. That's a strong message. We've rattled someone's cage."

Dorie nodded and separated from Ross. "Come in. What have you heard?"

Ross followed her back into the townhouse. "I was out at Joe's farm north of town. He was also interested in Trudy, but as a wife not a mistress. He said she turned him down cold. He's engaged to Emmie. Unlikely he would be murdering Trudy." He closed the door.

Dorie's phone pinged, and she fished it out of her bag. "Toxicology is back from Atlanta. It says she had ketamine in her blood stream. Her stomach contents included fried chicken and chocolate cake."

"Mama's Café most likely." Ross smiled. "Care to meet me for lunch there tomorrow?"

"Sure. Remember we're headed to Mr. Andrews's in

about half an hour, too." Dorie absentmindedly unpacked her bag, laptop, notepad, and yellow page of suspects. "People will begin to talk."

"They'll do that anyway. I'd better go freshen up. Meet you outside in about twenty minutes." Ross let himself out.

Chapter 9

Threats continue …

The pizza delivery car was driving away as Dorie and Ross pulled into the driveway. Ross unfolded his body from Dorie's compact car.

"Why did we take your car?" Ross stretched. "The truck would be easier on my body."

"We didn't need the nursery truck in the Andrews's driveway." Dorie slammed her door.

"Are you saying you're ashamed of my truck?"

"'Course not. It's just too big for a subdivision driveway."

The screen door slammed on the front porch.

"Hey, you two! Pizza's getting cold." Mr. Andrews waved at them from the front steps. "And my wife is hungry."

Ross gestured to Dorie to lead the way. Dorie headed toward the house and felt Ross's hand on the small of her back. *Interesting.*

"Lilah's getting the pizza ready. Translation: removing it from the boxes and putting it on warm pizza stones, so it looks homemade and stays hot." Mr. Andrews shrugged. "It helps her feel better about herself, especially when there's company."

Dorie and Ross followed Mr. Andrews into the dining room and sat in the indicated chairs. Mrs. Andrews wheeled into the dining room with a pizza stone in her lap. Dorie hopped up and took it from her and placed it on the table.

"Anything else I can help with?"

"Thank you, Dorie. There's a pitcher of sweet tea in the refrigerator."

Dorie walked into the kitchen. The counters were standard height. The tea was on a top shelf in the fridge. How would a wheelchair-bound woman work in this kitchen? Dorie grabbed the pitcher and the second pizza stone, taking both into the dining room and setting them on the table.

"So, Ross, how's the nursery business?" Mr. Andrews passed the stone to him. "I need a few new trees in the back. Perhaps you could come by this weekend and make some suggestions."

"You have a beautiful kitchen, Mrs. Andrews." Dorie accepted the stone and chose a couple of slices of pepperoni. "I'm surprised that you haven't renovated it yet to accommodate your wheelchair. I guess that's pretty expensive though."

"Call me Lilah. It's not a problem yet. I can maneuver along the counters for now." She smiled a wide grin. "It's okay. I don't mind talking about my MS. I'm fighting for my independence for as long as I can."

Mr. Andrews cleared his throat, commanding attention. "For the record, I've offered to take care of the kitchen, but she refuses. Stubborn lady."

Ross nodded. "Can't blame her for wanting to stay as active as possible, right Dorie?"

First time he used my name. She nodded. "Of course. I'm glad you are able to still do what you like." Dorie passed the salad bowl, but her mind was churning. *Could Lilah have murdered Trudy?*

At the end of the evening, Dorie and Ross drove back

home in silence. Ross followed Dorie to her front door.

"What are you thinking?" Ross put his hands in his pockets. "I could see your mind whirling across the table."

"Could she have killed Trudy?"

"Seems unlikely. You said that Andrews never actually had a relationship with Trudy. Why would Lilah kill Trudy? Being pregnant with someone else's child is no threat to either of them." Ross shrugged. "It's late. See you later."

"Hey, Ross. You called me Dorie tonight."

"It's your name." Ross smiled. "Good night, News Lady, knock on the wall when you're getting in bed."

Once Ross entered his townhouse, Dorie jumped back in her car and drove over to Java Joint.

Dorie entered the coffeeshop and collapsed into 'her' booth in the back of the room. Weariness washed over her. Maybe she should have just stayed home instead of drinking coffee. She spied Angela moving toward her with a cup. She pulled her computer out and set it up.

Angela placed her regular mocha, double shot, next to her elbow then slid into the booth across from her. "How's it goin', Dorie? Doin' okay?"

"Just tired. I probably should be home."

Angela reached across the table and held Dorie's hand. "Ross can be exhaustin', no doubt. And this murder thing is awful scary. It can't be easy on you, bein' new in town and all."

Dorie took back her hand and sipped her coffee. "You're right. Being the new person in town doesn't make it any easier."

"How can I help?" Angela settled in. "There's not much business from now till close."

Dorie reached into her bag and pulled out the yellow paper with the list of suspects. "I don't know how to read some of these people. How can I tell if they are being truthful?" Dorie set the paper in front of her. "Give me a read on them."

"Sonny and Gina Goldstein. Sonny acts out doin' whatever he wants to do. Gina pretends she don't know about his 'adventures'."

Dorie typed while Angela talked.

"Ethan and Lilah Andrews. Ethan looks, but he wouldn't cheat on Lilah. She'd have no reason to hurt Trudy. Plus Lilah is too frail to stab anybody or climb in and out of the kudzu."

"That's what I thought too." Dorie typed in Angela's opinion. "What about Sharon and Marie at the *Beacon*?"

Angela shrugged. "They may be hard to get to know, but they are just cliquey. I don't think they'd kill anybody."

"They cut me dead every time they refuse to allow me into their circle." Dorie took a long sip of the mocha. A tear slipped down her cheek. "I am clearly too tired to be working."

"Sorry Ross bein' the way he is." Angela looked away.

Dorie grabbed a napkin to wipe her face. "What do you mean 'how Ross is'?"

"Closed down." Angela shook her head. "Not open to anyone or love."

"What happened?" Dorie had to pull information from Angela.

"Emmie and him were an item in high school. Ross got a great scholarship to study agriculture. Emmie wanted to go to college with him and have babies. Ross said 'no' and that was it for them."

"Surely that's not the only reason." Dorie stopped typing to listen more closely.

"Day of graduation from UGA. His grandpa didn't show up. His parents were already gone by then. As soon as he could, Ross moved out of the dorm and headed back to the farm." Angela paused. "Found him dead at the bottom of the stairs, all dressed up, ready to go to graduation."

"Oh, that's horrible!" Dorie finished her mocha.

"What's horrible, News Lady?" Ross's woodsy cologne announced his presence.

Angela jumped up from her seat. "Let me know if you need a warm-up, Dorie."

Ross slid into the seat beside her. "I went to your door, but nobody answered. Then I noticed the blueberry car was gone."

"Blueberry car? Let's not name my sweet azure ride a blueberry!"

Ross 'Mona Lisa' smiled. "Blueberry it is. I had a thought. Hilde has a thing for the mayor. Do you think Trudy's pregnancy and possible return to Daelin would threaten Hilde?"

"I think it would threaten Gina more." Dorie started packing up her computer and notes.

"Are you leaving?" Ross grabbed one of her hands. "Was it something I said?"

"Yeah, blueberry." Dorie scooted out of the booth and threw her bag onto her shoulder.

"Don't leave. I just tracked you down. I've been looking for you for a long time."

Dorie paused and looked at him. *What did he mean by that?* He seemed coy and somehow vulnerable. "I'll see you tomorrow. I'm not going anywhere."

She walked out to the parking lot to her 'blueberry' car sitting under the street light. The closer she came to it, the more she noticed something on the side of the car. Dorie fished her phone out of her bag and turned on the flashlight. Scratched into the side of the car were the words "Dorene, Go Home." Ross was right behind her when she collapsed, into his arms.

Chapter 10

Getting personal . . .

When she roused, Dorie was on the ground in Ross's arms. Chatter squawked from the police car with the flashing lights, and an ambulance was entering the lot. Crime scene specialists were photographing the car and taking fingerprints. As she tried to gather herself together, Ross's arms held her tighter.

"Stay down. The ambulance just got here. I want you to be checked out." His whisper tickled her ear. "Who knew your full name was Dorene?"

Dorie struggled to answer the question. "The *Beacon*, for tax purposes. Or anyone who wanted to do a little digging. Who would do this?" *Definitely should have stayed home.*

Angela and the EMTs reached Dorie about the same time.

"What happened?" Angela knelt down beside her. "Oh, no. Who would do this?"

The EMTs helped Dorie up and had her lie on the stretcher. While they checked her blood pressure and pulse, police officers were talking to Ross and Angela.

A police officer came over to the stretcher. "Lt. Riley McDonough. I'd like to ask you some questions. Would that be okay, Miss Dorie?"

She nodded.

"Who would do such a thing?"

"I don't know. Trudy Jakes's murderer, perhaps." Tears streaked her cheeks. "I also received a live rat in the mail at the *Beacon* today."

Lt. McDonough wrote diligently in his incident notepad. "Anything else unusual happen?"

"Not that I know of." Dorie turned to the EMTs. "I think I'm okay. Take all this stuff off me, so I can go home."

"Whoa, Dorie." Ross came running across the lot. "You should go to the hospital and let them observe you. You could still be in shock."

"I can set up a round-the-clock guard on a room at the hospital." Lt. McDonough agreed with Ross, talking to each other over her. "She really shouldn't be alone after two direct threats."

"No. I can sleep better at home. My car is damaged, not me." Dorie struggled to get off the gurney. "No thanks, guys. I can drive myself home."

"Actually, you can't." Lt. McDonough pointed at the tow truck pulling into the lot. "Your car is evidence for the time being. You'll need to arrange for a ride, or I can take you home."

"This day just gets better and better." Dorie escaped the gurney and sat on the curb.

When it looked like not one more vehicle would fit in the lot of the Java Joint, Ethan Andrews screeched into the lot barely missing the squad car. To Dorie, it seemed Mr. Andrews bolted out of the car before it even came to a complete stop.

"What happened? Are you okay? Who did this?" Mr. Andrews plopped down on the curb next to her. "I thought you were going home after pizza at my place. My police scanner woke me."

Dorie realized Mr. Andrews was wearing red plaid

pajamas.

Ross answered for her. "We went back. She dropped me off and then came here."

"Come home with me, Dorie. Lilah always has the guest room in readiness." Mr. Andrews reached out to her. "Take some time off."

"No, I'm fine!" Dorie pulled away from her boss. "I can go home and go to work. No one has hurt me. They're trying to scare me." She grabbed her bag and stood in time to see her car being loaded onto the flat-bed tow truck and headed for the police evidence lot.

Ross put his arm around Dorie's shoulders. "I have an idea. Let's get you out of town for the rest of the week."

Dorie looked at him and nodded. She found Lt. McDonough. "Can I go now? Ross is going to look after me."

"Stay in touch, Miss Dorie. We want to know you're safe."

"You've got my cell number, right? I always answer my phone."

With his nod, Ross and Dorie jumped into the truck and headed to Helen.

The twists and turns up the mountain were dark, and fog made the visibility difficult. The big nursery truck strained in several gears trying to pull the steep stretches. Dorie shrank into the dark green MacAvoy's Nursery hoodie Ross had offered her. As hot as it was, Dorie couldn't believe how cold she was.

As they pulled into the drive of Ross's mountain home, the old-fashioned yard light was all that greeted them. It was midnight, and Dorie's eyes could barely stay open.

Ross hopped out of the cab, came around to Dorie's side, and opened the door. "Do you need me to carry you in?"

Dorie shook her head. "I should be able to walk." She

yawned, then climbed down from the cab and crumpled to the ground.

He caught her on her way down and swung her up into his strong arms. Dorie threw her arms around his neck and held on. When they reached the porch, Ross set her on her feet, so he could fish his keys out of his pocket. After opening the front door, he picked her up and carried her over the threshold and up the stairs to the redecorated master suite.

Ross sat her on the bed. "I'll go down and grab you a cup. What else do you need?"

Dorie sank into the bed. "But where will you sleep?"

"College days futon in the living room." Ross rubbed the back of his neck and smiled. "I've got a big landscaping job tomorrow, which should take most of the day. I'll go get your bag and computer out of the truck. Don't tell anyone, but I have Wi-Fi. I'll leave you the password with your stuff next to the Ninja Coffee Bar."

Dorie started to protest, but Ross hushed her.

"You need time away. Think, research, and write. I'll bring up dinner when I'm done. There's soda, coffee, cheese, peanut butter, cereal. Bread's in the freezer. Right now, you need sleep. I'll be downstairs until about six if you need me."

Ross kissed her on the forehead and closed the door on his way out.

Dorie stripped down to her underwear and climbed into the queen bed.

Dorie woke to her cell phone ringtone "Morning Coffee Jazz." The ID read Ethan Andrews, and the time was 10 AM.

"Hello, I'm not at work 'cause you said I should take the day off." Her voice was edged in panic.

"No worries, Hudson. Just thought you should know

that Ross's greenhouse was torched this morning."

Dorie gasped. "We're getting close."

"Yes, ma'am. You're getting close. Thought you'd like to know. Be careful."

Chapter 11
Making sense of everything …

Dorie bounded out of the bed into the sunlit bathroom. On the sink was a plastic cup that wasn't there before. Ross came in while she slept? And a note: "Hope your day is restful. I'll check on your car. Relax. That's an order. R."

She texted Ross, "Heard about the greenhouse. You okay?"

Dorie waited a few minutes for a reply. Having not received one, she got in the shower.

As soon as she got out, she checked her phone. Nothing. She dried off and put her clothes from yesterday back on. Deodorant? Nope, unless she wanted to smell like Ross's woodsy cologne. Time to think camping.

Still no response from Ross. Where was he? Was he okay?

Dorie found another note on the coffeemaker: "Knew you'd be here. Eat something too. Neither man nor woman lives on coffee alone."

After starting the perfect cup of coffee, Dorie called him only to get his voice mail.

"MacAvoy's Nursery. This is Ross. Leave me a message."

"Ross, it's Dorie. Thanks for last night. Your house is

amazing. Hey, Ethan called and told me about the greenhouse. The good news is we're getting close. Let me know if I should get a rideshare down the mountain, so I can help you out." She hesitated. *Should she say "Love ya"? Nah.* "Call me back. I'm kinda worried."

Dorie hung up but wasn't satisfied. After she fixed the cup of coffee, Dorie toasted a bagel and headed out onto the deck overlooking the mountain and the valley below. She found a Bible in the chaise lounge with a sticky note attached. After setting breakfast on the side table, she read the note.

"If you find yourself here, you have found my favorite spot to have quiet time. My family Bible has records back to Scotland. Don't worry. It's safe on the screened-in porch. You can bring it in if it bothers you to leave it out. Rest in the Lord today. You can get back at it tomorrow, News Lady. R."

She sighed. Still no reply from him. She opened the Bible at Ross's marker, took that first satisfying sip of coffee, and began to read.

When her phone woke her, the Bible was on the deck, the bagel was mostly eaten, and the coffee was gone. Twelve noon.

"Dorie, it's Hilde. I noticed you and Ross didn't come home last night. Things going well?"

"Actually, Ross whisked me out of town to keep me safe. My car was vandalized, and I was threatened." Dorie's eyes misted over, and a knot in her chest indicated it was still painful and too soon.

"Oh no! Here I thought you were on a romantic evening together."

"No, we're not there ... yet. We work well together though. That's something." Dorie rolled her eyes. "What do you know about the greenhouse fire? Ethan Andrews called me this morning about it."

A pause of silence.

"Hilde, are you still there?" Dorie wondered what role Hilde played in this whole mystery. *Was she more involved than they had given her credit?*

"Um, yes. I don't know anything more than that. Gotta go." And she was gone.

Dorie stood and stretched. Apparently, she needed this break after all. Still no message from Ross.

Dorie grabbed the phone and stabbed another text to Ross. "Are you okay? How is your business? Can't you at least respond? I am WORRIED about you."

Almost as soon as the message swooped away, her phone rang. Ross.

"Hey, you! Are you okay?" Dorie found it difficult to keep the anxiety and tears from her voice.

"Hey, relax, News Lady. Everything will be fine. No worries. I'm standing on the edge of the parking lot behind the crime tape."

Dorie flopped into the chaise lounge. "Your business. Is this my fault?"

"'Course not, sweetheart." An awkward silence. "How do you like Chinese?"

Dorie took a deep breath and wiped at her eyes. "Chicken and broccoli with fried rice. Get egg rolls and sweet and sour sauce."

"Gotcha. I'll see you soon. Nothing more I can do here after all."

Dorie clicked off. *Sweetheart? Probably just a Southern thing. A girl can hope, though.*

When Ross arrived with takeout paper bags from the Shanghai Star, Dorie met him in the yard and took the bags. Ross reached out and gave her a quick hug.

"Enjoyed your spa time, News Lady?" Ross draped his arm around her shoulders.

Dorie laughed. "Right. I've paced the floor worrying about who keyed my car and sent me a rat and who burned your business to the ground. So, I guess I've got my steps in for the day. Oh, and one more thing, by the way, who killed Trudy Jakes and is all of this the same person?"

Ross squeezed her shoulders. "Darlin', you needn't be worried. Cars and greenhouses can be replaced or repaired. I figure we've got Trudy's killer worried."

"Exactly my point." Dorie avoided the terms of endearment Ross had begun using and shrugged away his arm as she reached for the doorknob. "This person burned down your livelihood, sent me a live rat, and removed my ability to get around. What's to keep him or her from physically attacking one or both of us?"

"We have to be diligent, circumspect, and cautious about our surroundings and company." Ross opened a cabinet and pulled out paper plates and napkins. "We've got each other's back, right?"

"My hero." Dorie batted her eyelashes.

Ross blushed.

As Dorie opened and plated the fried rice, meats, and vegetables, the aroma filled the farmhouse kitchen. If the food was as good as the smell, Shanghai Star would be on her quick dial. She was staying. No one was going to run her out of town. She'd just arrived, and this was her job. Plus, Ross was here, which was becoming more and more important.

"Why don't we move this feast to the deck?" Ross handed her a Coke.

Dorie took both Cokes while Ross dug out 2 cookie sheets to use as trays.

They each took a chaise lounge, balancing their Chinese take-out on ancient cookie sheets. At first, they ate in silence until the sun began to dip behind the mountain. Then the night became a veritable babble of evening forest sounds. Tree frogs, crickets, birds, and cicadas chirped and cried out.

"How did you enjoy the house today?' Ross reached

out to her and clasped her hand.

Dorie moved her hand, entwining her fingers with his. "The house is amazing, and the setting is peaceful and harmonic. I still wonder why you live in town. If you lived in Atlanta, it would take more time to get to a job than it does to drive down the mountain."

"It can be lonely. This place is good to spend time with the Lord or to work on things without interruption. Long spells of it make me melancholy." Ross turned toward her and clasped her hand. "With the right person, it could be heaven, a home away from the world."

"I can see that." Dorie waited for the explanation of Ross's mood. "What are you thinking tonight?"

"I know we've not known each other long. With you, Dorie, it could be heaven."

Dorie gasped. "But we're …"

"No, let me finish. It's taken me so long to work up the courage to speak." Ross held his finger to her lips. "My grandfather gave me my grandmother's ring to give to a special woman one day. Not a diamond but a garnet. Grandpa told me that I would know the woman who deserved them both, a garnet as well as the diamond. Are you that woman?"

"Not sure what that means, Ross." Dorie's tears streaked her face. "Garnet is my birthstone."

"A coincidence, or not. To me, it represents an understanding between us." Ross dropped to his knee. "I reserve the right to ask you another day to wear my mother's diamond."

"I don't know what to say." Dorie allowed Ross to take both her hands in his.

"Wear my ring, Dorie. It represents the unbreakable connection we share. A promise of a future together."

Dorie nodded.

Ross slipped the garnet ring onto her left hand, and they kissed. "Should we stay the night, separate, of course? Or should we hurry back to Daelin?"

Dorie smiled as she wiped her tears. "Should we be in a hurry to leave heaven?"

Then Ross laughed, his ginger stubble catching the light. "Heaven it is for six or so hours. Then we will rejoin the real world once again. Do you need a coffee before bed, my dear?"

"Hardly, Ross. My blood is sufficiently caffeinated. Who is our culprit?"

Ross stood and pulled Dorie into a snug spot under his arm. They looked out over the valley. "The mayor. Hilde. Someone we haven't thought of. I'm afraid we're targets now."

Dorie twisted the old-fashioned garnet ring on her finger. What did it really mean? More, who should she fear? Leaving heaven meant returning to the unknown dangers Daelin held.

Chapter 12

Coming into Daelin on a mission …

The big green nursery truck rolled into the apartment parking lot at seven A.M. Dorie hopped down, grabbed her computer bag, and hurried up to her front porch.

"Hey, girl, where do you think you're going?" Ross ran up onto her porch behind her. "You are not getting away that fast. That ring means I get a kiss good-bye." He bent to her lips and took possession of them.

"I bet Hilde is watching, Ross."

"Let her watch." Ross dipped Dorie and kissed her again. "I'm falling in love with you, Dorie. Any problems with that? Tell me before I'm lost."

"I need deodorant, Ross. And fresh clothes." Dorie tried to pull away. "No problems with falling in love. As long as we're lost together."

Ross smiled and hugged Dorie to him. "Get dressed appropriately, and I'll drive you to work. Then I'll go check on your car situation."

"Ten minutes." Dorie hurried into her townhouse before Ross stalled her again.

She noticed the curtain move in Hilde's townhouse. Her skin raised in goose bumps. What did Hilde know about ketamine?

Ross dropped her off at the *Beacon*, and Dorie settled

into her desk and chair. The newsroom hummed with activity: phones ringing, printers printing, her fellow newshounds talking, typing, and tracking their stories. Dorie wrote the guiding questions for any journalist on a piece of lined paper:

Who? Sonny, Gina, Hilde, an unknown individual.

What? Murdered Trudy, warned herself and Ross off.

When? June 1

Where? Daelin kudzu

Why? Trudy was pregnant, killer felt threatened.

How? Ketamine. Hid in kudzu.

Who has access to ketamine? Dorie googled it. Anesthesia used for horses by veterinarians. Available in ERs and surgery. How would someone get such a drug, let alone use it, to assist in murder? She set it aside to finish her piece for the week's new edition.

"Dorie, are you okay?" Sharon sat in the chair beside her desk. "We heard what happened to your car and to Ross's business."

Dorie sighed. "I think we're still shaken. Thanks for asking. How would someone get ketamine?"

"The easiest way would be at the horse show happening this coming weekend. It's an annual event. The steeplechase is in May, just before Trudy's death." Sharon fidgeted in her seat. "You know, Hilde is the mayor's representative for the horse show. And she's also having an affair with him."

Dorie leaned toward Sharon. "Do you think Hilde is a murderer?"

"Don't know." Sharon shrugged. "She's sure interested in Sonny, though."

~

The sirens woke Ross early the next morning. When he opened his eyes, flashing lights caused him to jump fully awake to the window. Police cars and an ambulance had pulled up outside the building. Dorie was in the back of the ambulance. He pulled on sweatpants and ran down the stairs and out the front door.

"What happened?" When Ross reached Dorie, he saw the gash in her forehead. "Who did this?"

Dorie reached for him, and he picked her up, pulled her to him, and hugged her.

"Ross, we need to take Ms. Hudson to the ER for stitches for her head."

Ross never wanted to let her go, ever. "Can I ride with her?"

"Family?"

"Fiancé."

Ross looked into Dorie's eyes and nodded in question. Dorie agreed with a nod. He released her into the ambulance. Then he climbed in after her.

"What happened?" Ross reached out and touched her forehead, which was still bleeding.

The paramedic procured another alcohol swab and a bandage.

"I was asleep, and a brick came through the bedroom window. The note said the same as the car, 'Go home, Dorene.'" She closed her eyes and wavered. "I'd like to sleep now." She lay down on the gurney, but she never let go of Ross's hand.

"Concussion protocol." The paramedic squawked into the walkie. "Excuse me, sir. I need to take some vitals."

When Dorie fell unconscious, Ross scooted down the bench to allow the paramedics to work. They rattled off statistics and medical words he had no reason to know but desperately wished he knew now. The siren pulsed in his head as the ambulance traversed Daelin, headed toward the local medical center. He touched her ankle and realized she was dressed only in summer pajamas. And he only in sweatpants.

"I can offer you a shirt, sir." The paramedic handed him a light blue surgical scrub shirt. Ross pulled it on over his head.

"Ross? Are you still here?" Dorie tried to reach for him.

"I'm here, Dorie."

The ambulance pulled into the Emergency Room bay and removed the gurney with Dorie into Daelin Medical Center. Ross held her hand until the nurse shooed him out of the curtained emergency area.

"We'll let you know something as soon as we know anything, sir. What's your name and relationship to the patient?"

"Ross MacAvoy, fiancé." The relationship title came out easier this time. He knew it was the truth of the situation. He would marry Dorie as soon as he could. He couldn't let her slip away from him like he had allowed the others. He certainly couldn't allow her to succumb to whoever was now threatening her life.

"Sir?" The nurse had touched his arm and was looking at him like he was unwell. "Take a seat in the waiting area, and we'll call you when you can come back."

"Take good care of her, please."

She nodded and whisked away, leaving him to stumble out to the mass of other people hoping their loved ones would be okay.

Chapter 13

Picking through the ashes …

Ross found himself without transportation back to Daelin because he'd climbed into the ambulance. They'd admitted Dorie. She had a concussion, as suspected, and a nasty gash sewn together with twenty tiny stitches to hopefully prevent bad scarring. She drifted in and out of consciousness. He paced the halls of the hospital in his sweatpants and borrowed surgical scrub shirt. He needed to do something useful. Sitting and waiting was not in his DNA.

"Ross! Yoo hoo! How's our Dorie?" Hilde ran toward him with an impossibly stuffed vase of daisies and wildflowers. "I came as soon as I was dressed appropriately."

Wow! Now he really did feel self-conscious about his apparel, or lack thereof.

"She has a concussion and stitches on her forehead where the brick hit her. Did you see anything?" In his mind he added, *Since you always have your nose looking out your window, you old busybody.*

"No, it was so early."

Ross checked for the time on his naked wrist. No watch either. Good thing he'd slipped on his Birkenstock sandals, at least. He looked at the nurse's station clock. Seven AM.

Hilde thrust the vase toward him. "I cut these at the mayor's garden."

"I'm sure she'll love them." Ross took the vase from her. "Why are you cutting flowers at Sonny's before 7 AM? Surely they are still in bed on a Saturday morning."

"Oh no, Sonny's been up for hours. Besides, they allow me the run of the garden, whenever I please."

Ross wanted to ask 'Why?' but he knew the answer would just make him crazy. "Thanks for the flowers. I'll take them to her room. She's really not conscious for visitors."

"I'm sure the person who threw that brick didn't intend to hurt Dorie." She crossed her arms, a defensive position. "Poor Dorie. She really has not had a good introduction to our fair town. Let me know if there's something I can do."

"Can you drive me back to the house, so I can change into something less comfortable?"

Hilde giggled behind her hand. "I can do that. I'll be in the waiting room while you take her the flowers. We can leave as soon as you return."

After Hilde dropped him at his town house, Ross showered and threw on jeans and a t-shirt. He grabbed a Pop-tart and drove over to the remains of his business.

The caution tape flapped in the breeze. The smell of smoke wafted through the hot, humid breeze. He lifted the tape and stepped under it into the ash. All of it was gone. The greenhouse, the cashier hut, even the decorative garden concrete statues were burnt and ashy. The land was all that was worth anything. He kicked a piece of charred stone that skittered across the lot.

The fire chief pulled up in his red truck and jumped out.

"Ross, whatchathink? Anything of value left?"

"Nah, Marty, it's a total loss. Only the lot is of any

value now." Ross shook his ginger head. "Hardly even worth rebuilding. Know anything about the fire?"

Marty squatted and rubbed ash in his palm. "Arson, fursure, Ross. Burned too hot for an organic fire."

"What about the chemicals in the hut? Wouldn't they have contributed to the flames?" Ross squinted into the sun.

"Nah, these chemicals were inflammatory and were spread throughout the greenhouse and the lot proper. Besides, this was a hot fire. Too hot for insecticides and herbicides." Marty stood and walked over to Ross. "This was a gasoline or kerosene fire."

Ross closed his eyes. The sting of smoke made them water. "Almighty God. Who would hate me so much to take away my livelihood?" Hilde's name popped to mind. Who else? She was the mayor's right hand. The mayor had fought him all spring and half the summer over the kudzu. Then he and Dorie had found Trudy in it. They'd exonerated Sonny for her murder for lack of evidence. Could Hilde be the culprit after all?

"Whatchathink, Ross? Any ideas?" Marty held his hand over his eyebrows and scanned the burned area. "Look, you can see the pour pattern amongst the ash."

Sure enough, the trail snaked up and down the aisles of trees and flowers and garden equipment. Not an accident at all. Arson. His heart broke at the destruction.

"Come over to the fire house tomorrow. I'll have ya a report to file with your insurance."

Ross extended his hand and shook Marty's. "Will do."

After Marty drove away, Ross got out his phone and took pictures of the mess, including that infamous pour pattern. This wasn't just a disaster. It was a crime scene. He'd take a trip to visit Riley today. Maybe they'd meet at Java Joint. He could take Dorie her favorite double shot mocha later.

Chapter 14

Sorting the evidence …

T he Java Joint was quiet this mid-afternoon when Ross entered to meet with Lt. Riley McDonough. Riley was already seated near Dorie's favorite table. He couldn't stop thinking of Dorie in the hospital, alone and possibly vulnerable. Ross needed to get back to her and see what the doctor had to say about her condition.

"Ross, over here." Riley called out and waved him over. "Angela's got your brew preparing as we speak."

Ross's glance to Angela was greeted by a nod and a one-moment finger salute.

Riley extended his hand to clasp Ross's. "A nasty business you and Dorie are caught up in. Vandalism, arson, assault. Not happy about Dorie's safety. Assume you are determined to protect her?"

Ross nodded as Angela placed a mug of his favorite brew on the table. "Angela, a mocha double shot for Dorie as I leave?"

"I was gonna to suggest just such a thing, love. How's she doin'?"

Ross took a sip of the coffee. "Unconscious last I saw her this morning. Wounded and concussed, the docs say."

"Such a thing. Who's doin' all this to her?" Angela wiped the table where Riley had dropped cookie crumbs.

"And the nursery fire is arson as well." Riley got out his notebook and started scribbling.

"Arson? Sheesh, Ross. Attacking you too?" Angela shook her head then hurried off to help another customer.

Ross held his forehead. A headache raged behind his eyes. "Any progress on the Trudy Jake's murder? Dorie and I have been doing some investigating. Apparently, we're on the right track, otherwise why are these things going on?"

Riley wrote more into the pad. "Still looking into it. Here's the police report for the arson. What you going to do now without the nursery?"

"There is a good question, Riley. It was never my dream to do landscape work. I wanted to work for the park service, but never had a reply to my application." Ross sighed. "I need to get out to the hospital. Thanks for meeting me."

Angela appeared at his elbow with a to-go cup for Dorie. "Give her my best, Ross."

Ross poked his head into Dorie's room. "You okay for visitors?"

"I've looked better, but since it's you, do come in." Dorie raised the hospital bed to sitting up position. "The doc says I can go home presently. You could take me home, if you like."

"Would you consider moving to Helen with me, until this is all done anyway? Not for inappropriate reasons, for your safety. And mine as well. I think we need to remove ourselves from Daelin until this is resolved. I don't have a business to run anymore, and you can work from there." Ross took her hand and touched the garnet ring. "I didn't say I was your fiancé in a spur of the moment desperation, you know."

"I know." Dorie grasped his hand. "I didn't nod for no reason as well. However, they have urged me not to sign any documents or drive until the concussion has resolved. I may need to revisit that decision later."

Ross laughed. "Fair enough. I'll not press my advantage until you are completely well. Helen?"

"Seems like a good idea."

After Dorie was checked out of the hospital, they returned to the townhouses and packed essentials for a stay in Ross's mountain home.

~

Dorie woke in Ross's master bedroom to the sound of a chainsaw. Her head still pounded as she stumbled to the bathroom. *Oxycontin or Tylenol? Tylenol, I need to work.* She popped the lesser painkiller and opened the window to see the source of the sound. Unable to see what was happening, she threw on her Virginia Tech sweatshirt and capris and headed carefully down the stairs in bare feet.

She stepped out onto the wraparound porch. Kudzu vines had been pulled down around Ross's grandfather's truck. Ross, clothed in jeans and no shirt, wearing noise canceling headphones, wielded the chainsaw with a vengeance. Dorie stepped from the porch and tiptoed through the grass to within an arm's length of him. She tapped him on the shoulder and stepped back quickly.

Ross whirled around with the chainsaw, battle-ready. When he saw Dorie, he shut down the chainsaw and ripped the headphones from his ears.

"I could have hurt you!" He set down the equipment and rushed to hug her. "How are you this morning? Did I wake you? Can I fix you a cup of coffee?"

His sticky, sweaty skin, infused with his woodsy cologne, pressed against her, was heady. Or perhaps it was still the concussion that made her head spin and not want to ever let him go. His ginger stubble raked across her face as he kissed her.

"You are crazy, Ross." She kissed him back.

"In love with you, News Lady." He kissed her again. "Don't take this the wrong way, but I need to let you go or I'll break my promise of 'no inappropriate behavior.' You look beautiful and at home here, with me."

She released him. "What are you doing?"

He slipped on his t-shirt. "Something I said to Riley yesterday reminded me. I applied to the National Park Service before graduation but had not received a reply. Then Grandpa died in that fall down the stairs, allegedly to go back to retrieve my graduation gift. But he didn't have the keys to the truck in his hands or pocket."

"That's odd." Dorie held his arm as they headed for the house.

"Yeah. I figured he'd been in the truck then forgot the gift." His voice choked. "I vowed not to disturb the truck and let the kudzu take it over."

They entered the kitchen. Ross started the process of making coffee in his fancy brewing machine. Dorie settled at the table, resting her head against the wall.

"He knew how much I wanted that Park Service job. What if he was bringing the letter to me? What if it's been in the truck all this time?" He brought her a cup of coffee and doughnuts he'd apparently picked up in Helen that morning.

After breakfast, Dorie ran upstairs to get dressed appropriately, and Ross headed back into the kudzu.

Ross hacked away at the kudzu. The July humid mountain air caused him to peel the t-shirt off again. After another hour, the truck was free of the persistent vine.

Dorie joined him in the yard. "What can I do to help?"

"I was just ready to open the door." Ross removed his headphones. "Pray. It's a little like opening his grave to me."

Dorie took his arm. "Together?"

Ross nodded and opened the door. The remembrance of his grandfather's Old Spice wafted from the cab. It brought tears to his eyes, which he wiped away with the back of his hand. He stepped into the driver's seat. The keys were in the ignition, just as he had suspected. He turned the key. The truck growled. He tried again. On the third try, the engine sputtered to life.

Dorie cheered. "Not bad for being buried in kudzu."

"Better than Trudy got."

Ross was solemn. He looked around the cab for mail. He ran his hand into the space between the seats. Dorie climbed in on the other side and checked the space behind the seats. Nothing.

Ross put the transmission into Drive, and the truck groaned forward into the sunlight. He reached up and pulled down the visor. An envelope fell into his lap. The return address was the National Park Service. He put the truck back into Park and turned off the ignition. Ross pulled out the keys, to the truck, to the house, to the shed, all on a UGA key fob that he had given his grandfather.

"Open it, Ross." Dorie placed her hand on his bare shoulder. "What does it say?"

He was almost afraid to find out what he'd missed due to his grandfather's fall. Ross stuck his finger under the dried-out glue and pulled it open. He unfolded the brittle paper.

"Dear Mr. MacAvoy, We are pleased to offer you the job of land management ranger in the Chatahoochee Forest along the Appalachian Trail...." Ross stopped reading.

"Oh, Ross. Your dream job." Dorie grabbed his hand. "I'm so sorry."

He dropped his head onto the steering wheel and squeezed her hand.

"You should call them Monday morning and see if there's any way you can still accept the offer or reapply for a new one."

At the end of the weekend, Dorie and Ross packed up their essentials to return to Daelin.

"Are you sure this is a good idea, Sweetheart?" Ross stood at the bottom of the stairs. "You are probably still in danger."

"I don't know about that. If I hadn't moved my bed so we could tap on the wall at night, my bed would not have been where the brick landed." Dorie came to the top of the stairs. "So I guess that makes it your fault I was hit by a brick."

"Don't make me come up there." Ross gave her a menacing look, climbed the stairs by twos, then grabbed her at the waist and swung her around. "Don't take this the wrong way, but I've enjoyed the time we've been here together."

"Me too." She kissed him playfully and tried to escape from his embrace.

"Are you ready for the next ring?" he whispered into her ear. "I don't ever want to be apart from you."

Dorie's insides fluttered. "Maybe that should wait until you talk to the Park Service."

"That won't change how I feel about you." He released her and knelt at her feet. "Marry me, Dorie Hudson. Let me love you and care for you. Live in this house with me as husband and wife."

"Yes, Ross." Today she could give him that answer. But what if he got a job someplace else?

Ross ran into the bedroom and returned with an old, battered ring box. He popped it open. A beautiful diamond solitaire ring was in the box with a matching wedding band.

Dorie moved the garnet to her right hand after removing her college ring. She offered her left hand to him. He slipped the diamond on the appropriate finger, leaving the wedding band in the box. A perfect fit.

"Are you sure you feel well enough to face whatever is happening in town?" Ross placed his backpack in the back of the crew cab.

"It will be fine. Whoever it is hasn't killed me yet." She handed him her overnight bag. "The window is fixed in my bedroom."

"I don't think this is brilliant, News Lady." Ross helped her into the truck.

"I feel fine. Plus, I still have a job to do." Dorie buckled her seatbelt. "Besides I have a plan."

Chapter 15

Gathering info from coffee and cinnamon rolls . . .

While the last K-cup drained into the transfer cup, Dorie finished icing her famous cinnamon rolls. Well, famous in her family anyway. She packed the half-and-half in her thermal tote, then poured the last cup into the large Thermos and packed it too. Then she slipped a recorder into the zippered pocket where most people stow an ice pack. There were things she needed to know.

Dorie wrapped the rolls in plastic wrap and settled the tote on her shoulder. A glance at the kitchen clock, just about eight, assured her that it was early enough, but not too early. She shifted the pan with the rolls to her hip while exiting her townhome. The sunrise was just painting the Daelin horizon. Resolutely she turned to the right and walked the few steps to Hilde's front door. Dorie inhaled deeply then smoothly exhaled.

Hilde responded quickly to the knock on her door.

"Dorie, what a surprise." Hilde welcomed her into her pink and paisley abode. Her floor length rose robe swished the peach carpet as she hurried to take the pan of rolls from Dorie. "These rolls smell divine."

Dorie handed her the rolls then set the thermal tote on her two-person bistro table. "We kept saying we'd get together for coffee, but it never was arranged. I thought a spontaneous arrival might give us some 'talk time' after all."

"I do have a few minutes to gab and eat these rolls." She dragged her finger through the icing and tasted it. "Hmmmm. I can put on a pot right now."

Dorie pulled the Thermos and half-and-half from the tote. "No need. I brought the Joe too."

"I'll get mugs then."

While Hilde bustled about her small kitchen, a mirror image to Dorie's, Dorie flipped on the mp3 device in the tote. She settled the tote bag on a bench under the window of the breakfast nook. To call it a breakfast room would have been too generous. Stacks of the *Daelin Beacon* lined the walls.

Hilde returned with the mugs, spoons, and sugar bowl. "Here we are." She took over hostess duties, pouring the coffee and serving the cinnamon rolls. "I'm meeting with Sonny shortly to discuss a rescue mission for the homeless in Daelin."

"Homeless? In Daelin?" Dorie didn't need to feign surprise. She'd recently written an article about the amazingly few homeless in Daelin.

"You might have to go north to see them, but be assured, they're there." She fixed her cup. "So, what's up so early on a Monday?" Hilde shifted her weight onto the bar-height chair.

Dorie cleared her throat. "I wanted to understand better the town dynamics. You know, who's sleeping with whom? Who is related to whom? Who could possibly want to kill Trudy Jakes?"

Hilde nearly choked on her coffee. As it spewed with Hilde's cough, Dorie ran for a paper towel to help clean up the coffee on the table and on Hilde's robe. Hilde sputtered and coughed some more while waving her off.

"What did I do? Is the coffee bad?" Dorie stood at the ready with the paper towels. Clearly, she'd touched a nerve.

"I'm okay." Hilde continued to sputter and cough. "Caught … me… by… surprise."

Dorie took a seat again. "You said you were the one to talk to about anything."

Hilde blew her nose and wiped down her robe. "So I did. Where should I start?"

"Tell me about Trudy, her friends, lovers, family."

Hilde coughed and took a sip of her coffee and a bite of cinnamon roll. "So good, Dorie. Trudy had many friends. Fact is, no one disliked her. She also had many men friends, if you know what I mean."

"Like who?" Dorie sure hoped the recorder was working. She tried to remain loose and casual. Her nerves were stretched thin. She mustn't let Hilde know this was on the record. She took a sip and cut the roll into pieces. "Glad you like the rolls."

"Guess you heard about the mayor. Sonny and Trudy had a thing going on. It was hot and heavy 'til she decided to move to Atlanta. Told Sonny he wasn't her Mr. Right, and she needed more than a married man. It made him so mad. How dare she hurt him like that." Hilde stabbed the cinnamon roll. "Sonny's a proud man. Trudy didn't deserve him."

"Who else felt like Trudy was disrespecting Sonny? Not just you, right?" Dorie held her breath, waiting for an answer without an attack.

"Look at the time. I need to be somewhere. Thanks for the coffee and rolls. I've got to change. Can you see yourself out? Don't forget your things."

Hilde was out of the room before Dorie could process her response. Dorie gathered her Thermos and half-and-half and put them in her tote, then she picked up the half-empty pan. Why was Hilde so interested in Trudy and Sonny? Who else might gain from Trudy's death if she was already moving away?

"I'm leaving, Hilde. I'm just next door if you think of anything else to help me."

A muffled call from the bedroom excused Dorie, so she left.

As she stepped onto the sidewalk, the door opened at 1248.

"Good morning, Ross."

The sun glinted in his eyes as he looked her way. "Your beauty blinds me this morning, News Lady. Are you consorting with Ms. Hilde today? Already? So early?"

Dorie laughed and turned under the shade of her door. "Better? You can see me more clearly then."

Ross laughed. "What does the great knower know today?"

"More than she's told anyone. Do you have a moment to listen to our conversation? Can I tempt you with cinnamon rolls and coffee?"

"I have a few moments. Can I take your stuff?"

Dorie handed him the pan and shifted the tote to him. She then fished out her keys, admitting them into her townhome. "Sit while I warm these up and get my recorder." She popped the rolls into the microwave then gathered the recorder from its secret place. "Hopefully this worked."

She propped it on the table and started it from the beginning. Their conversation was clear. While Ross listened, she made his favorite Dark Magic K-cup and scooped two freshly heated rolls onto a plate. She joined him at the table and listened to the recording. When it finished, Ross reached across the table for Dorie's hand.

"Promise me you will not be alone with that woman again. Bang on the wall or call 911 next time she comes over. She'll be coming for you next."

Dorie gave Ross an incredulous look. "Come on, Hilde? She's not dangerous."

"And that's how she killed Trudy. Trudy never suspected that she'd angered her when she planned to go to Atlanta and then changed her mind."

"Changed her mind? When did you hear that?" Dorie drew back from him. "Explain."

Ross stood and walked to the chair beside her, placing his hand on her shoulder. "Dorie, she had moved to Atlanta, but she missed tiny Daelin. I ran into her at Java. She was homesick and imploring Mr. Andrews for her job back."

Dorie gasped. "No."

He squatted beside her and took her hand again. "Mr. Andrews told her that he had hired someone already. She stayed with Hilde for a while. Then she was gone again. Promise me you will stay away from Hilde."

Dorie pulled her hand away and stood. "No one told me this before. You are scaring me. Are you really thinking Hilde is the murderer? I don't think she could pull this off alone. And why am I promising you to stay away from the ghost we've been chasing? Why don't you just say what you're trying to say?"

Ross shrank back into the chair beside her. He ruffled his hair and smoothed down his beard. Finally, he stood. "You know I care for you. I thought you knew that."

Dorie lifted her left hand, so the light caught in the diamond on her hand. She walked into his arms. "I said yes, didn't I?"

His arms encircled her waist. "I couldn't stand it if I lost you."

"I love you too." Dorie stretched to reach his lips and kissed him gently. "I already said yes to forever together."

He held her tight. "I never dared dream you could love me. I only hoped and prayed."

The cuckoo sounded the hour.

He looked into her eyes. "I've got to go meet Sam

Ridley about a tree. Promise me you'll stay safe."

"I'll do my best, Ross."

She kissed him again, and he returned the kiss with passion.

His phone rang. He pulled it from his jeans and hissed under his breath.

"It's Sam. I've got to go. Gotta pay for that house renovation after all." He extricated himself from their awkward embrace, then returned for another kiss. "For you. And me. For us." His face grew a deep crimson. "I'm hoping we'll spend the rest of our lives there. Together."

Ross rushed out the door leaving her with a promise for forever and a fear about tomorrow. With whom should she share the recording with next? Dorie cleaned the kitchen and took the rest of the cinnamon rolls with her to the *Beacon*. Devoured within minutes, she was the toast of the office, for those few minutes anyway.

"Hudson, are you in there causing a commotion?"

"Guess so, Mr. Andrews." Dorie carried a cinnamon roll she'd saved for him to his office. "I saved you one before the feeding frenzy began."

"Thanks." He took a bite leaving icing on his mustache. "What's new in the Trudy story?"

"Well, I'm suspecting someone, but I have no evidence to prove it. Just a suspicion and a recording." Dorie paused. "Is anyone covering the horse show this weekend?"

Mr. Andrews checked his clipboard. "Yep, Marie is assigned that. I can swap assignments, so you can do it, if you like."

"I think that's where the Ketamine came from that drugged Trudy."

Mr. Andrews chewed on the end of his pencil. "Let's allow Marie to cover the horse show. You go do some snooping for 'color commentary' on the important

people in the show."
　　"Yes, sir."

Chapter 16
News from Atlanta ...

Dorie couldn't think of a time when she had voluntarily shopped for a hat, much less a Fascinator hat, like women wore to a royal wedding, in order to attend the horse show.

Since acquiring this assignment, Dorie had learned that the steeplechase was held in late May, about a week before Trudy's death. Her next stop was to the veterinarian who oversaw the horse show and steeplechase.

"What do you think of that hat?"

The voice of the clerk broke into her thoughts. Dorie glanced in the mirror again. This Fascinator was composed of a burgundy swath of mesh bows with burgundy and navy-blue flowers and feathers. Feathers! On a burgundy 'saucer' attached to a headband. So that's how those la-de-da royals kept their hats on.

"What color is your dress, Miss Dorie?"

"Dress? I need a dress too? I have a skirt and tank top I thought I'd wear."

"Tsk, tsk, tsk. No, no, no. You must have a fashion dress. That is the uniform of the horse shows and steeplechases, the Derby and the Ascot." The clerk snatched the hat from her hair and balanced it back on the display rack. "No point buying the hat until you know what dress you'll be wearing."

"I'll buy the burgundy one." Dorie grabbed the hat back off the rack. "How much?"

"It's marked down to eighty-two dollars."

It took all her self-control to keep her gasp internal. The summer had been quite expensive already between renting the townhouse, finding required furniture, buying a car and a new laptop, repairing her car, and a hospital bill.

"Ok. Wrap it up." Dorie dug for her lone credit card. Was a hat a business expense? It was amazing they didn't charge for the box too.

With her fancy hat box in hand, Dorie stepped out onto the sidewalk on Main Street. The fancy-dress shop was nearby. Couldn't hurt to look in the window, could it? In the window was a flared rose sundress with navy and gray flowers on the bottom. Could she be that lucky? Sure enough, the one in the window was the only one in the store, but it fit. Another hundred dollars on the card.

By the time she arrived at Mimi's for lunch, her credit card was smoking, but she'd be properly attired on Saturday. She hoped Ross had found time to meet her there. As she entered the dining room, Ross jumped up from a corner table.

"Did you find what you needed for the horse show this weekend?" Ross kissed her and held out her chair.

"After a fortune spent, I did." Dorie took the menu and scanned it. "Maybe I should just have water."

"Now, I can pay. I'll get my insurance money soon." Ross sipped his Coke. "Besides, I have interesting news."

"About the Forest Service letter?" Dorie grabbed his hand. "What did they say?"

Ross pulled his hand back after a squeeze. He chose a muffin from the basket, split it, and buttered it. "The problem is the Chattahoochee Forest has no openings for the rest of the summer."

"Then what can they offer you?"

"They have some short-term work in various places that I can fill in until the Chattahoochee has an opening." He took a crumbly bite of the muffin. "I'm headed to Atlanta tomorrow to meet with a guy named Glenn."

"But I thought you were going to the horse show with me, so I don't get killed?" Dorie frowned. "Marie won't have my back, you know that."

"Just stay away from Hilde, and you should be fine." Ross patted her hand and continued eating the muffin, creating crumbs all over the table cloth. "You can call me if you have a problem. This afternoon I'll be polishing my resume´ to have available for Glenn."

Dorie jumped up from the chair and picked up her purse. "Enjoy your lunch. Drive safely to Atlanta."

"Dorie, wait. Come back."

She waved at him and escaped the restaurant and the disappointment by jumping in her rental car and driving to Java Joint for a chicken salad croissant and her double-shot expresso mocha. How much did she spend there? Surely that was a business expense. The corner booth was practically her office.

When she returned to the *Beacon* after lunch, Marie flounced up to her desk. "What color are you wearing tomorrow?"

"Burgundy and navy blue."

"That's good. I'm wearing yellow and orange. We won't match, which is good if you're going to be poking around." Marie folded her arms. "You don't want to stick out."

"No, I don't." Dorie narrowed her eyes at Marie's back as she walked away. *What was her deal? Could she have been jealous of Trudy? And of me, somehow? Could she be the murderer after all?* Either way she'd be alone, with Ross in Atlanta.

Dorie watched Marie the rest of the afternoon. With whom she spoke. When she was on the phone. How she interacted with others. Paranoia had set in. And she was screening her phone calls from Ross. How dare he leave her to face a murderer?

Dorie arrived home with Shanghai Star takeout, her computer bag, her dress bag, her hat box, and the mail. Opening the front door was a struggle, ending up with the mail on the floor and the hat box across the room. She dropped everything except the food into the chair by the door and headed for the kitchen. The smell of barbequed ribs permeated her townhouse. Ross must be grilling.

Dorie opened the sliding patio door to confirm the smoke was coming from Ross's patio. He probably expected her to drop everything and join him. She twisted the garnet ring. How was it that everything she'd bought for tomorrow's horse show matched it? She slid the door closed with a thud. How could one man take over her life so completely in such a short period of time? And now he was planning to leave her, following the job he never got, to wherever it took him.

Dorie plated her takeout and popped a Coke. She took it into the living room and turned on the TV for some mindless activity. She continued to ignore Ross's texts and calls.

"Ribs?"

"Cherry pie?"

"Come on, Dorie. I'm sorry."

"I love you, Sweetheart!"

"Forgive me?"

"Don't go to bed angry!"

"Darling?"

Dorie turned off her phone.

She hung the new dress and clipped the tags. She shuddered at the price again. She opened the hat box and clipped the tag, even on sale too much. Dorie dug in the closet and decided on some strappy, burgundy low heels in case of murderer alert.

Nine cuckoos announced bedtime for this night. Dorie prepared for bed.

After she turned out the light, she heard it.

Tap, tap, pause, tap, tap, tap.

Good night. I love you.

Since they'd been back in Daelin, Dorie and Ross had developed this tap code on their shared wall to say good night. Dorie turned her phone back on and called Ross.

"Dorie! Are you okay? I'm sorry. Don't give up on us."

"Calm down, Ross. Yes, I'm angry that you are leaving me when I need you to watch my back. More than that, where do you think you're going after you accept whatever short-term assignments that they assign you?" Tears of frustration pricked her eyes. "You said forever. How can you leave me so soon?"

"Oh, Dorie, I'm not leaving you. I'm driving two hours south to meet with a guy with a proposition. I'll be back tomorrow evening."

"But will I? What if Trudy's killer succeeds in murdering me?"

Chapter 17

Horse show happenings …

Dorie opened her door just as Ross was beginning to knock.

"Good morning. You look beautiful." Ross took her in his arms. "I am not abandoning you. We will have dinner tonight together. We'll know more then."

Dorie nodded. "Okay. Waffle House for breakfast?"

"As long as you wear that feathery hat thing while you eat your waffles." Ross tousled the feathers in her Fascinator. "You won't be alone. Riley is going to look out for you today."

After Waffle House, Dorie kissed Ross good-bye. While Ross headed down I-75 toward Atlanta, Dorie drove her rental car to the county fairgrounds. The horse show drew folks from all over northeast Georgia. The parking lot was already filling up with trucks, horse trailers, RVs, SUVs, and every kind of car you could imagine.

The milliner was correct about the hats and dresses. Dorie felt downright underdressed. And the shoes! Stilettos at the fairgrounds? The ground was soft from an overnight rain. Her shoes may not be *au rigueur*, but they were practical. And she was an investigative reporter after all.

Dorie made her way to the veterinarian's tent, side

stepping puddles, litter, and people. The tent was full of people, animals, tables, and chairs. Dorie spotted the medicine cabinet immediately. Dr. Jan was busy with a child's scraped knee.

"Dr. Jan, how goes it?" Dorie threaded her way over to the vet's work space.

"Busy already, Dorie." She gave the boy a candy and sent him on his way. "The medical tent is just getting set up. If they get the human emergencies, then I can focus on the other animals here. Nice get up, girl."

"If I could get away with a white jacket, tank top, and jeans, I would have done that too." Dorie took a seat across the table from her. "Did you inventory the ketamine?"

"Always. Especially when I take it out of the clinic." Dr. Jan grabbed her clipboard. "Like I told you yesterday, the only discrepancy I've had was in May during steeplechase weekend."

"The weekend before Trudy was killed." Dorie nodded and her Fascinator dislodged. "You'd think that this expensive bit of fluff would stay in your hair, wouldn't you?"

Dr. Jan laughed. "How do the royals do it?"

"They have people to make it stay in place, then they smile and wave even though it's giving them a headache." Dorie peered into the glass cabinet door and tried to rearrange the hat.

"Tylenol?" Dr. Jan handed her a packet of medicine and a cool bottle of water.

"Thanks, I need it already. Gonna be a long day."

Dorie stood as a man ran into the tent. "Dr. Jan, one of the horses is acting like it has heatstroke."

"Don't worry. My veterinary assistant Joe will watch over the medicine cabinet." Dr. Jan grabbed a bag and headed toward the makeshift stables.

Dorie wandered out of the tent while scribbling on a

notepad. After a few tests of the microphones and amps, country music blared across the fairgrounds from the stage. Horses were still being backed out of their trailers. Food kiosks were set up in a haphazard plan – barbeque, kettle corn, roasted corn on the cob, cotton candy, funnel cakes, and hot dogs. Children zigzagged through the crowd carrying food and drinks, even at 9:30 AM. In addition to the food, horse show ring, and music, crafts of all kinds were on display.

The July heat and humidity were also already causing Dorie to sweat. She spotted Hilde and decided to see what she was up to.

Hilde pointed at her clipboard and waved her pen around in the air. "No, no, no. According to the mayor's plan, this booth must be six inches farther to the left."

"It ain't moving, Miz Hilde. I done got my electric hooked up and all my stuff set up. It's stayin' the way it is." His booth was filled with tooled leather belts, humongous belt buckles, purses, backpacks, and wallets. His tent also held a machine for personalizing leather on site. The man wore overalls, quite a contrast from Hilde's fancy duds and spike heels.

"The dress code was quite specific, Berle. Your outfit does not fit the horse show's air of refinement."

"Ain't changin' that neither." Berle went about setting his wares on the tables, leaving Hilde fuming.

"Some people will find themselves without booth space next time." Hilde scribbled on her clipboard and nearly ran into Dorie. "Dorie, you look lovely. I wish others had taken this event more seriously."

"I can already see that you and the mayor have put a lot of work into this event." Dorie wanted Hilde to know she was there but didn't want to antagonize her. "Your outfit is divine."

"I see you had to settle for the dress in the window at Martin's." Hilde swished her tulle skirt with obvious pleasure. "I had to go to Atlanta to find this. Doesn't it just say garden party?"

If the garden party was held by June Cleaver in the 1960s, perhaps. "Of course," Dorie kept her thoughts to herself.

"Where is your beau Ross this morning? I thought I saw the two of you together, as always."

"We had breakfast together this morning. He has a job interview in Atlanta today. He'll be back by dinner this evening."

"Gotta go." Hilde stalked off, clipboard in hand, to harass some other booth renter.

"Miss Dorie." Berle signaled to her to come over. "I got something for you. Trudy was a niece of mine. I appreciate you working to discover her killer."

He dug in one of the boxes and pulled out a burgundy leather backpack purse. "I know you're haulin' your laptop around while investigatin'. This might help you some."

Her name, Dorie, was tooled into the strap.

"Thank you, Berle. It's beautiful." Dorie put her notebook into the bag and slung it over her shoulder.

Toward noon, Dorie had seen pretty much what there was to be seen. She purchased a barbeque sandwich, chips, and a Coke and found a seat on an outer picnic table where she could still see the entrance to the vet tent.

As she half-dozed in the sun, Dorie suddenly was nuzzled mid-back. She turned quickly and discovered a beautiful white and fawn greyhound who had escaped the Greyhound Adoption Meet and Greet booth. She grabbed the leash, so she could walk her back.

"Hello, sweet girl. What are you doing wandering about alone?"

The greyhound nuzzled her hand and placed her head in Dorie's lap. Dorie clasped her "ADOPT ME" collar and hugged her head.

"You are beautiful. Maybe you are exactly what I need while Ross is gallivanting around the country chasing his dream."

"Miz Dorie, thank God. I thought we'd lost Lilith." The lady running toward her gasped for breath. "I'm Kathy. I've been chasing her all through the fairgrounds. I was afraid she'd come to harm."

"Lilith found me." Dorie handed her leash to the lady. "What do I need to do to adopt Lilith?"

"Come back to the Meet and Greet tent, and I can get you the application form."

"Don't give her away. I think she's just what I need." Dorie rubbed Lilith's head and her ears. "I'll come back with you now."

Dorie walked back to the Meet and Greet with Lilith and Kathy.

"Oh, praise the Lord. You found my Lilith girl." The older lady grabbed her leash and pulled her to her.

"I'm Dorie. Lilith found me."

"Liz." She put Lilith back in her crate under the tent with the fan going full blast. "It's hard on the dogs being out in the sun so much. They all need water, shade, and cool air."

"Liz, I need to adopt Lilith."

Dorie left the Meet and Greet tent with the paperwork in her bag and a promise that they'd be holding Lilith for her. She headed back to the vet tent to check the log and the ketamine stash.

Dorie walked into the vet tent, but no one was there. The cabinet was open. A vet assistant rushed in.

"What's happening?" Dorie waved at the man.

"A horse went down." The man grabbed a bag and hurried to the entrance. "Dr. Jan's having to put it down."

"The ketamine?"

"Can't say. Gotta go."

Dorie looked into the cabinet. All the ketamine was gone. But how much had Dr. Jan taken and how much was missing? She picked up the clipboard and scanned the entries. No ketamine had been checked out until now.

The prick and the blow happened at the same time. Before Dorie could turn around, her world went black.

Chapter 18

Coming back from Atlanta …

R oss pressed the button on his phone. "Siri, call Dorie on cell."

The continual ringing greeted his call once again. Finally, the voice message clicked in, "Hi, this is Dorie. You've missed me. Leave your name, number, and news scoop, and I'll get right back to you."

"Dorie, it's Ross again. I'm nearly back to Daelin. I've been calling for nearly two hours. I'm getting worried now. I'm almost home. I'll find you, love. Don't worry, I'll find you."

He pressed the accelerator harder and upped his speed by ten miles per hour. He had to get to her before it was too late.

Soon he arrived at the Daelin exit. He drove straight to the police station.

"Riley!" Ross burst into the station yelling at the top of his voice. "Riley, you got to help me find her."

A police officer came into the waiting area. "Sir, you need to calm down. Lt. McDonough will be right with you."

"Don't tell me to be calm. My fiancée is missing. Lt. McDonough was supposed to be keeping her safe while I was gone." Ross choked. "If something's happened, I don't know what I'll do." Ross dissolved into anguish and dropped into a chair. "It's not his fault. I should have been here."

The officer got him a cup of water from the cooler. "Here, drink this. It will help."

Ross took a deep, ragged breath, then drank a sip of the cool water. "What am I going to do?"

Riley entered the waiting room and motioned him to come with him. Ross staggered after him through the cubicles and waiting areas.

Ross grabbed Riley's shoulder and pulled him back to him. "What's happened to Dorie? Tell me straight. She hasn't answered her phone for the last two hours."

"Trust me, I know." He pointed to a burgundy backpack. The leather strap read "DORIE." Riley reached in and pulled out Dorie's phone. "No point calling this phone right now."

"I've never seen this backpack before. Where did it come from?"

"Berle, the belt maker, gave it to her for her hard work on Trudy's case." Riley sat behind his desk and gathered paper and a pencil. "I know you and she have been trying to solve this case without us. What have you discovered?"

"Where did you find it?" Ross fixated on the backpack because his head and heart hurt trying to think about what could have happened.

"It was in the vet tent with her hat. Someone apparently injected her with something..."
"Ketamine."

"Probably. They dropped the syringe and left all her belongings right where they injected her. Then there are drag marks to the parking lot."

"Fingerprints on the syringe?"

"We're working on it right now, Ross. That is our job, y'know."

"We thought it was Hilde. No one else made any

sense."

Riley made some notes. "Why did you think it was Hilde?"

"Riley, we don't have time to play games. Dorie could be dying or dead." Ross's head began to whirl. "Don't you understand? I can't lose her."

Riley signaled to another officer. "Ross, this officer will find you a quiet place to lie down. I'm going out to look for her." Ross began to protest. "No, you can't help us at this stage. Lie down. I'll come back to get you in about an hour. Let us do our job."

During his grumbles and protests, Ross nearly passed out. Riley finally convinced Ross to let him do his initial investigating while he rested.

Ross woke to the sound of voices in the hall. He dragged himself out of the cot.

"What have I missed?" Ross stretched and tousled his hair.

Riley handed him a burger bag and directed him to the break room. They sat down at a table. Sgt. Junior Osbourne plunked money in the soda machine and got Ross a Coke.

"Did Dorie have her car at the horse show?"

Ross took a bite of burger. "Yes. Wait. No. She was still driving a rental car."

"Good to know. We've been looking for her blue car. Which rental company? Most have a GPS retrieval system." Riley yelled into the incident room. "Junior, check the rental company GPS."

"How can I help?" Ross sucked down the Coke. "Have you checked Hilde's and Dorie's townhomes?"

Riley nodded. "Where else could they be? Hilde's car is still at the fairgrounds."

"Kudzu? But not where Trudy was." Ross tapped the table. "Could they be up at my house near Helen? There's kudzu there. 'Course there's kudzu all over

Georgia."

The clock on the wall ticked while Ross and Riley thought.

Junior stuck his head in the room. "Lieutenant? The rental company says the GPS must be whacky 'cause it says it's near Helen."

Ross was out the door before Riley could caution him.

Riley grabbed his arm while Ross was unlocking his truck. "Wait, Ross."

"You can't stop me. I have to save her." Ross shoved Riley away.

"I was going to suggest you ride in the patrol car. I have sirens."

Ross pocketed his keys. "Let's go then."

They were halfway up the mountain in the dusk and the rain. The radio crackled to life.

"Dispatch to Lt. McDonough."

"McDonough here. Go ahead, dispatch."

"Helen PD has been briefed and is arriving on scene. They report a car in the kudzu and are approaching with caution."

"Roger, dispatch. Relay that we'll be arriving with support in fifteen. Ten-four."

"Can't you make this car go any faster?"

"Not on rain slick, curving mountain roads, Ross. Don't worry. Police are on scene. They know what to do."

Ross forced himself to sit back in the seat. His heart pulsed with the siren. His teeth hurt from clenching his jaw. She had to be okay. What good was the perfect job without Dorie? He rubbed the back of his neck. Had he caused her to be in danger by chasing a past-tense job?

Chapter 19

Saving Dorie …

Awareness dawned slowly for Dorie. It began with sound. *Hilde's voice. The sound of the car. A song on the radio. In the distance, a siren?* She realized she couldn't move her body. *Must be ketamine. Is this the end?*

Her vision returned, though blinking was out of the question. Darkness surrounded her, but slowly light from the car interior helped her see Hilde. *So this is it.* But she was okay with it. At peace. She'd miss her relationship with Ross. She'd miss having Lilith as her dog. But there was heaven and Jesus, the final benefit of Christianity.

The sirens grew closer.

"I'm sorry, Dorie. I really am, but you've snooped too much into it. I can't have you messing with Sonny and his reputation." Hilde put Dorie's hands on the steering wheel. "It's right you should die here. At Ross's house. Mind you, it might make Ross a little sad. Don't you think those sirens will save you. All I need to do is push just a bit more special K, and you'll slip off to sleep."

Dorie heard the spin of gravel from under the tires and the sirens come to a stop. Hilde was filling the syringe with a death's dose of ketamine. Nothing she could do now. Wait, her fingers had sensation against the steering wheel. Dorie slid her hand down to the horn and pressed as hard as she could.

The horn blast shocked Hilde into dropping the syringe and vial.

Blinding light filled the car.

"Hilde Behan! Helen PD! Come out of the car!"

Police approached the vehicle, guns drawn.

Hilde searched frantically on the floorboard and came up with a gun. She held it to Dorie's head.

"Drop the gun, Hilde. Put your hands outside the car and drop the gun."

The bullhorn gave Dorie a headache. She shook all over as sensation returned to her body.

"Exit the car with your hands up."

"I can't. I need to finish this…finish you."

Hilde raised the gun again and cocked it. A shot rang out in conjunction with another siren entering the scene.

Blood trickled down Dorie's arm. Dorie was still conscious, but Hilde was not.

~

Ross jumped out of the police cruiser before it had properly stopped. He scrambled past the police line before anyone could stop him. The ambulance arrived as Ross reached the car.

"Dorie. Are you okay?"

Riley pulled Ross away from the car. Officers moved Dorie onto the ambulance gurney. Ross grabbed her hand. Dorie squeezed it as hard as she could. Ross squeezed back. The paramedics loaded her into the ambulance, and Ross climbed in with her.

The EMT hung a bag of saline while the other talked with the hospital.

Another ambulance took Hilde's body to the medical examiner's lab.

Chapter 20

Resolving affairs …

T he next time Dorie awakened, she was in the hospital, again. Who knew investigative reporting could be so dangerous in a sleepy little town in Georgia? Ross slept in the chair beside the bed.

A contingent of doctors and nurses entered the room, startling Ross awake.

"Good morning! I'm Dr. Rahesh, and these are students from Atlanta doing rounds with me today. Is it okay to share your case and prognosis with them?"

"Sure." Dorie's voice was raspy.

Ross grabbed her hand and pulled the chair as close to the side of the bed as he could.

"How are you feeling today, Miss Dorie?" The doctor flipped open her chart. "Miss Dorie was apprehended using a strong dose of ketamine. You can see the site here at the base of her neck." He released the snap at the top of the hospital gown and leaned her forward. "She was hit with some force, as you can see from the bruising around the puncture wound."

The group gathered in to look at her. She squeezed Ross's hand as hard as she could. Mild panic began in the pit of her stomach.

"Who can tell me the proper use of ketamine?" Dr. Rahesh asked the group.

Eager hands raised. He chose someone who began rattling off a medical definition, use as a precursor to anesthesia, and possible side effects.

"Excellent. What happens when someone abuses ketamine?"

Another ambitious student rattled off statistics about use on the club scene. Many technical terms, which Dorie didn't know or remember, ended with the word "death." Ross jumped from his chair to get closer.

"True, true." Dr. Rahesh scribbled something onto a notepad. "You, Miss Dorie, are a very lucky woman. Your kidnapper is dead, and you are not. We want to observe you for other side effects for the next few hours. With any luck your young man can take you out for dinner on the way home."

Ross sat down on the side of the bed. Dorie scooted over, and he moved farther onto the bed.

"I almost lost you." He put an arm around her and held her hand with the other. "I should have gone to the horse show with you instead of going to Atlanta."

"How did your interview go?" Dorie tried to turn to see his face, but pain shot up her back.

"Surprisingly well. They have offered me a job in the Chattahoochee Forest, but it doesn't start until next summer." He shushed her as she tried to speak. "I know, not what I need for now. However, they will hire me full-time to help out in other areas of the country that have a specific need."

Dorie felt her hopes fade. He would be gone until next summer. Who knew what would transpire between now and then?

"Where and when do you start?" She tried to control the quiver in her voice and willed the tears to stay unshed, though her heart was breaking.

"California. I fly out Monday. I'll be helping the park service plant trees in land that was burned in the recent fires."

Dorie reached out for the hand he was holding and took the diamond ring off her finger. "You'll be wanting this back then."

"No, I don't want it back. Keep it on that finger." He placed it back on her left ring finger. "The only way I want this off of this hand is when I replace it with a wedding band." He took her hand again.

"But what does it really mean? Is it a promise that someday, when you actually live here, we'll get engaged? I barely know you, and you don't really know me. And you're leaving." The tears refused to stay put and spilled down her cheeks.

"No, it's more than that. I love you, Dorie. You are my soulmate. I knew it the day you threw coffee on me. I just know that you are the wife God wants for me."

Dorie's heart was so full, she could barely breathe. Or was it residual effects of the ketamine? "I think that too. But just as I found you, you need to leave me."

"Sir, ahem, we do not sit on patients' beds." The nurse breezed into the room, adjusted the blinds, and then waited for Ross to comply.

"I'm not going anywhere until she can go home." Ross's jaw was set in determination. "I don't want to spend any time we have separated."

The nurse pursed her lips. "The rules are in place for patient safety."

"Well, I plan on keeping her safe for the rest of our lives."

Dorie waved the nurse off. "It's okay. I'm fine with him here."

She harrumphed, turned heel, and left the room. As soon as she was gone, a rap at the door got their attention.

"Come in," Dorie answered.

"Riley." Ross jumped out of the bed and shook

Riley's hand. "Without your work, Dorie might have died last night."

Riley's face turned red. "I was just doing my job. Glad to see you looking better, Miss Dorie. I thought you'd like to know that the police are releasing Hilde's body for burial. Word is that Mayor Giles is paying for her funeral."

"But Riley, Hilde couldn't have moved me from the vet tent to my car by herself. Hilde may be dead, but there's another out there involved in this assault."

Machines by Dorie's began screaming resulting in the arrival of several nurses.

"What is going on in here? Out, out, out."

Riley and Ross were both shoved from the room. One nurse lowered the bed to bring down Dorie's blood pressure and heart rate while the other worked to silence the alarms which were almost as upsetting.

"You need to rest Miss Dorie. The ketamine is still in your system. If you want to go home this afternoon, you need to lay back and rest. How do you feel?"

"I have a headache."

"I'll check your chart about when you can have some Tylenol."

One nurse pulled the blanket up to her chin. The other closed the blinds to block the summer sun from the room.

When the nurses left Dorie's room, Ross followed them to the nurses' station. "Can I go back in with her?"

"One of you can go back in after I give her some medicine. Please remember that her job in this place of business is healing, not solving crime or writing front page news." The nurse placed her hands on her hips. "If I have to clear her room again, you will be barred from visiting her. That goes for Lt. McDonough as well."

Ross and Riley sat down in a waiting area while they waited for Ross to get the okay to return to Dorie's bedside.

"Would it have to be a man, or could it be another woman?" Ross watched as Riley chewed on Ross's thought.

"Got anybody in mind?" Riley took out his incident pad and scribbled in it. "Did you and Dorie have any other viable suspects?"

"Gina? What about that officer that guards the mayor?" Ross searched his mind for someone they'd not thought of yet. "Wait. Could it be…?"

"Who?"

Ross cocked his head and put his hand to his mouth. "It's something Sonny said when I had him hauled off to the station the other week. He said, 'The police answer to me in our small town.'"

"You think someone on the force is involved?" Riley shook his head. "But who?"

Chapter 21

Finding the accomplice …

As Dorie sat on the patio of her townhome, the scraping and thudding of movers on both sides of her shattered the otherwise peaceful morning.

Ross was moving his things to the house in Helen. Next week he planned to move her things there as well, so she could keep a watch on the property while he was gone and save her rent money for other plans, like a wedding one day.

Sonny's movers were taking Hilde's townhouse apart. Word was that he was donating most of the furnishings to the domestic abuse shelter. The reporter in her wondered about the connection between Sonny, Hilde, and domestic abuse. Marie was covering that story since Dorie was officially on medical leave. Still, Dorie felt sorry for Gina. How could she abide not one but two mistresses, one pregnant, and both funerals paid for by her husband? Also not her story.

Her story was attending the funeral of the woman, her neighbor, who tried to kill her. And waving good-bye to her quasi-fiancé, then moving into his house in the mountains, without him. Life was truly stranger than fiction.

Ross rapped on the gate to the patio area from the alley. "Can I come in, Sweetheart?"

"Of course." Dorie stood to greet him. Her knees gave, and he helped her back into her chaise lounge chair. "How's it going?"

"Good. All my stuff is on the nursery truck." Ross wiped the sweat from his forehead with his bandana. "Ben's going to drive it up to the house. He'll take it back to his shop after we unload it. I'll have Grandpa's truck to drive back down the mountain."

"Good thing Ben bought the truck from you." Dorie stood carefully. "Graveside service is at two at Loblolly Pine Cemetery. Can I get you a drink? Coke? Coffee? Water?"

"No, let me get you something. Are you sure you should be at this mockery of a service? She nearly killed you, and she killed Trudy. I don't get your need to be there. She died in the car next to you." Ross gently pushed her back down. "Coke? Anything else? Then I have to go unload the truck."

"Just a Coke." A refreshing breeze escaped from the air-conditioned townhouse as Ross opened and closed the sliding door. Could she actually attend that funeral? Would her legs hold her up? Would she feel the panic in her stomach again? She'd be okay someday, but he was right. Today wasn't that day.

~

After the weekend, Dorie had her blueberry car back and was cleared for light duty. Translation: Sit at her desk, and research and write stuff. Riley had given her a police roster with personnel files to glance through for any remembrances from the night of the assault. When the bell rang as she entered the office, everyone, even Sharon and Marie, stood, clapped, and cheered.

"Welcome back, Dorie. So glad you're here." Mr. Andrews pulled back her chair for her. "Everybody back to work."

He settled into the chair next to her desk. "Is it true

you're looking at one of Daelin's finest as Hilde's accomplice?"

Dorie moved the basket of fruit and flowers from her desk to give her a place to work. Then she pulled the files Riley had given her from her tote bag. "I really don't remember anyone. It just seems obvious that Hilde had muscle to move me that far."

"Makes sense. Well, let us help catch the SOB who hurt you. We stick together when it's one of our own." Mr. Andrews stood and gave Dorie a shoulder hug. "Are you still in the townhouse? Lilah wants to send dinner tonight."

Dorie nodded. He went on toward his office, leaving her to field the concerns and questions of her fellow reporters.

Once the welcoming had ceased, Dorie pulled her folder on the Trudy murder from the desk drawer and placed it atop the police folders. She leafed through her notes and clippings. Finally, she looked through the pictures Greg, the photographer, had taken during the press conference. That's when she saw it. The guilty look in his eyes and the handkerchief to wipe away tears. Dorie picked up the phone and called Riley.

"Was the gun Hilde's or someone else's? And have you got fingerprints back from the gun, the syringe, or the car?"

"Good morning, Dorie. Feeling better?" Riley laughed. "Yes, we do have information about all those things. The forensic team spent the weekend tearing the crime scene and the rental car apart. We're just about to make an arrest if you want to send Greg over. If you have an idea who it is, place a slip of paper with the name in an envelope and bring it with you."

"Will do. See you soon." Dorie motioned to Greg. "Grab your stuff. There's about to be a big arrest." She sent a quick text to Ross, gathered her necessities, and headed for the police station.

Ross met her in the police parking lot. "What's going on, News Lady?"

Dorie handed him her envelope with her guess. "I think this person is about to be arrested. Don't peek yet."

Riley opened the door and sent them down the hall to the break room. The entire force had crammed into the small space.

Riley hushed the crowd. "So, I have an important announcement. The forensic team has determined who Hilde Behan's accomplice was. We have enough proof to arrest someone now."

Foot shuffling and a low murmur met Riley's remarks.

Riley took out his cuffs. "Chief Dennis White, please stand. I am arresting you on the attempted murder and assault of Dorie Hudson. You are also accused as an accessory in the murder of Trudy Jakes. In addition, Sonny Giles is also being arrested for the murder of Trudy Jakes and the planning and execution of the attempted murder of Dorie Hudson. You have the right to remain silent …"

The room burst with sound as Riley slapped on the cuffs. The chief made no response. He hung his head as a police officer took him back to the cells. As the crowd simmered down, a pair of officers brought Sonny into the station in cuffs as well and booked him into the cells.

Riley joined Ross and Dorie in the waiting room where Gina Giles wailed.

"Let me see your guess." Riley opened the envelope and pulled out a picture of the chief headed down the hall with his handkerchief wiping his tears. "You saw it too."

Ross nodded. "That and what Sonny said the morning I called 911. 'The police work for me.'"

"You have the exclusive scoop here and pictures

thanks to Greg. Go write it up. Andrews will want it on the frontpage tomorrow." Riley handed the picture back to Dorie. "Now we've got to establish a new chain of command. I might be chief of police."

Dorie hugged Riley. "Couldn't be happier. Let me know when you fill the hierarchy so I can print that too."

Chapter 22

Concluding this chapter …

It was Labor Day when people from church, the paper, and the police force helped move Dorie's belongings from her townhouse to the house in Helen. They set her bed up in an extra bedroom that Ross had cleared out, repainted, and laid new carpeting. The third bedroom upstairs became her office with an antique desk she'd found on a shopping trip in Helen. It also had new carpeting and a fresh coat of paint. It needed shelves and file drawers, but she could have those delivered later. For now, she could work from Helen most days and go into Daelin as necessary.

Meanwhile, Ross was manning the grill and smoker out in the backyard. The newly installed privacy fence allowed Lilith the run of the festivities, as well as attention from all the guests. Music played from the covered deck above the yard. Lawn darts, croquet, and corn hole were in process in different parts of the area.

Dorie was in the kitchen replenishing food for the crowd. They'd bought potato salad, macaroni salad, chicken salad, watermelon, all kinds of chips, and plenty of Coke products. *Tomorrow Ross heads for California.* That thought reverberated in her brain even as she served and smiled for their guests. Before long she'd be alone in this house.

The screen door slam introduced Riley's entry.

"Hey, girl, you shouldn't spend the whole party in the kitchen. These are your guests as well." He leaned against the counter. "I am so glad we got here in time to save your life."

"Have I thanked you for that yet?"

"Not necessary, Dorie." Riley plucked a carrot stick from the garnish tray. "Actually, I'm feeling quite jealous of my friend. He has this lovely place as well as a lovely lady. And he's fool enough to leave her alone." He chomped the carrot and watched her as she moved around the kitchen.

"But look at you. You're now Captain and Chief of the Daelin Police force." Dorie avoided the area where Riley stood. "You're a good catch yourself, Riley."

"Guess she hasn't appeared on the scene yet. I'll go see if your catch needs any help at the grill."

Dorie breathed a sigh of relief at Riley's departure. She couldn't let him think she would cheat on Ross while he was gone.

~

Dorie waited while Ross checked his luggage at the airline bag drop in the Atlanta airport. Feelings of abandonment threatened to overflow. She was determined to make the best of this time. Six months of separation was nothing compared to a lifetime together.

Ross shouldered his backpack and turned toward her. His smile helped her panic, a bit anyway. The lowering sun through the airport glass shone in his ginger hair and stubble. When he reached her, he wrapped his arms around her and squeezed her tight.

"This isn't the end of our story, News Lady. It's just the close of this chapter."

"That is so corny, but so comforting." Dorie sniffled back tears.

"Hey, we have Facetime, texting, Skype, Messenger, Facebook. It will still feel like I'm on the other side of the wall." Ross kissed her tears.

"Except I'll be in your bed in your house, alone."

Ross laughed. "No, you'll have Lilith with you. And all those things are ours now. Plus with you there, I won't worry about all my hard work wasting away."

"So I'm just a housekeeper now?" She grimaced at him.

"Hardly. Just don't get mixed up with anymore psycho killers, promise?"

"I'll do my best. You be safe in the wilds of California." Dorie didn't want to let go, but the time was coming. "You better go on and get through security. I love you, Ross MacAvoy. You come back to me."

"Cross my heart, Sweetheart. I love you, too." Ross released her and walked backwards while crossing his chest with a large air X. Then he signed 'I love you.'

Dorie blew him a kiss and signed 'I love you' as well. The garnet ring caught the light.

He turned and headed for the security line. She watched until his ginger head disappeared in the crowd. It was time for Dorie to head back to Helen and Daelin, find another story to report, and fill the time until Ross came home to stay.

About the Author

Diane E. Tatum began writing in grade school with short mystery stories, a play performed by her sixth-grade class, and a dictionary of supernatural beings. High school found her writing serial fiction with her friends, including developing characters and plot lines through hand-written notes. Her first book, *Gold Earrings,* is an outgrowth of a short story written in a high school creative writing class. More historical Christian novels are in the works; most are part of an historical series. *Mission Mesquite* is a contemporary novel inspired by the Mesquite Rodeo in the Dallas area.

Diane has written many assigned pieces for Lifeway, including curriculum, devotions, and assigned articles for leadership magazines. She has also branched out into freelance publication including poetry, leadership articles, a story for teens, and helps for parents. In addition to her writing career, Diane taught middle school language arts for 11 years. She has worked as a church youth group leader and worker since 1981. She also serves as adjunct professor of English at Motlow State Community College.

She is loved and supported by her husband, Ken, and their 2 sons and daughters-in-law. Her four young grandsons are a joy to them all.

Bible Study/Book Club Discussion

"Woe to you, teachers of the law and Pharisees, you hypocrites! You are like whitewashed tombs, which look beautiful on the outside but on the inside are full of the bones of the dead and everything unclean. In the same way, on the outside you appear to people as righteous, but on the inside, you are full of hypocrisy and wickedness."
Matthew 23:27-28 (NIV)
The lesson of the kudzu is the same for us: beautiful on the outside, dead and ugly on the inside. It doesn't matter how much makeup we apply, how much jewelry or fashionable clothing we wear, how much plastic surgery we have, or how much weight we lose or gain. Until our inside is pure, we are not beautiful. It's a façade requiring a change of heart that only a relationship with Christ can achieve.

1) Which characters would you consider worthy of the title Kudzu Sculpture? What ugliness hides within?

2) The ugliness inside us can be past sins, attitudes, ego, fear, disinterest in others' needs, lack of self-respect, violence (verbal, physical, internal), or allowing the past to destroy your future. What is kudzu hiding in you? Take time to consider this question and talk with God about it. Confess sins. Make your

relationship right with God. Make your human relationships right as well.

3) Sonny was a deacon and had 'even baptized people', yet clearly, he was a poor representative of the church. He paid for the funerals of Trudy and Hilde. How much blame for those deaths do you think Sonny should be responsible? Should he still be mayor of Daelin? What role do you think Gina played in these deaths? [Let me know what you think; it is an ongoing series! tatumlight@gmail.com]

4) Ross and Dorie become engaged very quickly in this book. Their relationship becomes long distance for the next six months. What do you think will be stressors on their relationship? Will their relationship survive?

5) Who is your favorite character in this book? Why?

Ezekiel saw a Valley of Dry Bones. God asked him if these bones could live. My New Testament response is, With man this is impossible, but with God all things are possible. No matter how dry our bones become spiritually, God can raise them up again to serve Him. Don't let the kudzu win!

The following is a Bible study written by my husband concerning the dry bones.

"Dry Bones" A Mystical Vision

By Ken Tatum
Ezekiel 37:1-4

The hand of the LORD was on me, and he brought me out by the Spirit of the LORD and set me in the middle of a valley; it was full of bones. [2] He led me back and forth among them, and I saw a great many bones on the floor of the valley, bones that were very dry. [3] He asked me, "Son of man, can these bones live?"

I said, "Sovereign LORD, you alone know."
[4] Then he said to me, "Prophesy to these bones and say to them, 'Dry bones, hear the word of the LORD! [5] This is what the Sovereign LORD says to these bones: I will make breath[a] enter you, and you will come to life. [6] I will attach tendons to you and make flesh come upon you and cover you with skin; I will put breath in you, and you will come to life. Then you will know that I am the LORD.'"
[7] So I prophesied as I was commanded. And as I was prophesying, there was a noise, a rattling sound, and the bones came together, bone to bone. [8] I looked, and tendons and flesh appeared on them and skin covered them, but there was no breath in them.
[9] Then he said to me, "Prophesy to the breath; prophesy, son of man, and say to it, 'This is what the Sovereign LORD says: Come, breath, from the four winds and breathe into these slain, that they may live.'" [10] So I prophesied as he commanded me,

and breath entered them; they came to life and stood up on their feet—a vast army.
[11] Then he said to me: "Son of man, these bones are the people of Israel. They say, 'Our bones are dried up and our hope is gone; we are cut off.'
[12] Therefore prophesy and say to them: 'This is what the Sovereign LORD says: My people, I am going to open your graves and bring you up from them; I will bring you back to the land of Israel. [13] Then you, my people, will know that I am the LORD, when I open your graves and bring you up from them. [14] I will put my Spirit in you and you will live, and I will settle you in your own land. Then you will know that I the LORD have spoken, and I have done it, declares the LORD.'"

Ezekial's mystical vision of a valley filled with long-dead bones is one of the most spectacular of the entire Bible. The reader is impressed immediately with the desolation and hopelessness of the situation. Most of us do not like cemeteries anyway, but confronted with vast numbers of bones simply scattered about on the ground is more than any of us would want to see. How could anything positive be gleaned from such a sight?

But, the good, even great, news is that what is hopeless to us finite, mortal humans is humdrum to God. As Jesus told his disciples, "with God all things are possible" (*Matt 19:26*). As Ezekiel soon discovers, God can take those bones and reassemble them into not only individual persons, but assemble the persons into a mighty (but still dead) army. Then, just to complete the point, God finishes His work by breathing life into them. One more reminder that even life itself is a gift from God! What an awesome image of the eternal God's power! When we are feeling truly hopeless we have a God who is not only always in complete control, but also has the power to change everything and to even bring good out of death.

So, there you have it. The lesson from this vision of the valley of dry bones is the power of God to overcome anything. Even the hopelessness of the Jews' exile to a faraway land is not too much for Him.

So, that's it. Good Bible lesson, short, sweet, and to the point. Right? Maybe, maybe not. Is God showing us something else in this desolate valley?

Is everything always what it seems at first glance? Ezekiel was pretty sure he was looking at a place of desolation. Most of the Israelites had seen a plentiful land with their eyes when they spied out Canaan, but saw only giants and huge fortresses with their hearts. Which was it? Obviously it was both physically, but when Caleb looked through God's eyes he saw only the blessings of God's provision.

The Jews exiled to faraway Babylon saw the loss of everything they thought they had accomplished in conquering Canaan. Their homeland, their temple, all gone. How could they ever again be a proud nation. Did they not remember the mighty power God had exercised bringing them across the Red Sea, through long stretches of desert, overcoming fierce hostile nations, and bringing down the walls of Jericho? Were their eyes deceiving them or were they just being realistic?

In the New Testament Jesus pointed out that our human vision can also deceive us the other way. The people saw the scribes and Pharisees as the ultimate men of God. They knew God's scriptures backwards and forwards. Not only did they know those words they also made it a point to obey every one of them, right down to the smallest letter! So when Jesus came He must have also thought them great. Right? No, He called them "whitewashed tombs" (*Matt. 23:27, NIV*).

Why do we paint something white? Because it looks clean, pretty, and undefiled. We usually try to make our cemeteries look nice and pretty and often new headstones are white. So we say "isn't that a pretty place." But would you want to live there? I don't think so. It's a place for dead people and old bones. So we look at a neatly trimmed and freshly painted place and say "how nice!" But is it really a place we want to live in, or is it actually a cemetery. Is it a beautiful work of art? Or is it hiding something dreadful and hideous; maybe even merely covering scenes of death and desolation?

So can we depend on what we see being what is really there? Are the eyes God gave us faulty?

The eyes God gave us originally are good (*Genesis 1:31*). But those eyes are physical ones for the physical world. They are limited to such and therefore can be deceived (*Luke 11:34*). God has far clearer sight. He looks within and not merely at the obvious (*1 Samuel 16:7*).

Matthew 19:26
Jesus looked at them and said, "With man this is impossible, but with God all things are possible."
Mattthew 23:27
"Woe to you, teachers of the law and Pharisees, you hypocrites! You are like whitewashed tombs, which look beautiful on the outside but on the inside are full of the bones of the dead and everything unclean.
Genesis 1:31
God saw all that he had made, and it was very good. And there was evening, and there was morning—the sixth day.
Luke 11:34
Your eye is the lamp of your body. When your eyes are healthy, [a] your whole body also is full of light. But when they are unhealthy, your body also is full of darkness.
1 Samuel 16:7
But the LORD said to Samuel, "Do not look at his appearance or at the height of his stature, because I have rejected him; for God sees not as man sees, for man looks at the outward appearance, but the LORD looks at the heart."

The next part of the story:
The Gemini Conspiracy

Chapter 1

Java Joint was jumping this night. Funky music on the old-time juke box. Strobing lights pulsed on a makeshift dance floor that no one ever used. Best coffee in town.

Dorie Hudson practically owned the table in the corner, her office away from the *Beacon* offices. She usually shared the space with her favorite nursery owner. She closed her laptop. Tears ran down her cheeks. She closed her eyes in hopes the tears would stop.

"One café mocha, extra shot. Hey, what's going on?" The barista wrapped her arm around Dorie's neck. "What did Ross do now?"

Dorie took the napkin and wiped her eyes. "Oh, he's happy working for the Forestry Service in California. He says its temporary, but his emails say otherwise."

"At some time, he'll figure out that happiness in Georgia is better than trees."

Dorie nodded, and Angela went back to work. Dorie started keying in her latest article before deadline.

The Java Joint bell over the door jangled as a tall cop entered the coffee shop.

"Hey, Lieutenant Riley! Espresso dark and black?" Angela had a gift of remembering every customer's regular order.

"You got it, Angela!" Riley wandered over to Dorie's table. "How goes it, Miss Dorie?"

Dorie looked up and wiped the tears off her face.

"Hey, Riley. Have a seat."

The thin man slipped into the booth. His gun clunked against the table. "Sorry 'bout that, I'm on break. Gotta get back to it after my espresso." Riley smiled. "You look like you've been crying, my girl."

Dorie smiled. "My girl?"

"Someone needs to take care of you. I'm taking you on. I'll watch after you."

Dorie laughed. "I'm a big girl. I don't need a bodyguard."

Angela brought Riley's steaming cup over. "Enjoy. Stay safe out there, Riley."

"There's hardly any crime in Daelin, until Miss Dorie came to town."

Riley's walkie squawked to life. "Break in at Records office. Captain, you available?"

"Ten-four, Joey. I'll head over there." Riley shoved the cup of espresso toward Dorie. "Have this on me. Just don't blame me if it keeps you up all night."

Dorie smiled. "No problem. I'll be up a while anyway. I'll be here until Angela kicks me out. Swing back through if you have time."

Riley nodded and headed for the door.

"Wait!" Dorie closed the laptop. "Can I follow you over?"

"For you, you can ride with and run the lights and siren."

Dorie turned to pack up.

"Nah, leave it. I'll make sure it's okay, Dorie. Go, play cop." Angela waved her away.

Chapter 2

Daelin was a quiet community nestled in the north Georgia mountains. In the dark, it seemed unoccupied. It was hard to think that there would be crime here, except for the murder Dorie'd uncovered with Ross. Now a break-in in the records office. Dorie had never ridden in a police car. Riley ran the flashing lights, hoping to catch the thief in the act.

The glass in the door was broken, and the door stood open. Records were strewn over the floor. Dorie stepped gingerly over the scene

Riley put on latex gloves and threw a pair at Dorie. He began checking the back door for evidence. "Don't touch anything without gloves. Don't move anything until forensics gets pictures."

As though conjured, the forensic van pulled up outside just then.

"Riley, were you born here in Daelin?" Dorie examined the antiquated drawer system. Only one drawer had been disturbed: the records labeled Mc. "Why do you think the only drawer dumped is the one your birth record was in?"

Riley shrugged. "Can't imagine why. This looks like vandals. We'll get prints off the drawer and the entrance."

"Is it okay if I gather and sort these records?" Dorie pointed out the large index cards.

"Knock yourself out. Just don't touch anything that the vandal touched in case we can get prints."

Dorie found an empty box in the recycling and began sorting the records. Crime scene personnel began dusting for prints, taking photos, and inspecting the scene for any blood evidence around the broken glass.

After an hour of noisy, focused business, the records office began to quiet. The crime scene specialists had left with their samples, cameras, and cases. Riley and Dorie were the only ones still on the scene.

"How goes it, Dorie?" Riley sat down across the table from her. "Anything missing?"

"Actually, yes. Two cards are missing. All the cards are numbered sequentially. When were you born, Riley?"

"June 12, 1985."

Dorie made her puzzled face. "That's what I guessed because yours is one of the cards missing. The other one is the same day with a last name that starts with Mc. Know anyone with the same birthday?"

Riley shrugged. "No, I don't guess so. It could be someone who has moved away."

"Why would someone take your birth card and the one closest to it? Do you have a twin? June 12 is in the sign of Gemini, you know."

Riley laughed. "I think Mama would have told me something like that. Still it's a little creepy. If you write a story about this, you should leave out those details for now."

Dorie nodded and stripped off her sweaty latex gloves.

The first rays of sun crept over the mountain.

"Could you drop me by the Java Joint? I've got to pick up my stuff and my car. Maybe I can grab a couple hours sleep before showing up at the *Beacon*."

"I would be delighted, Miss Dorie. Angela is openin' up about now. I could sure use the caffeine." Riley opened the squad car door for her and shut it after she was settled.

~

Dorie tried to sleep the allotted two hours, but she kept tossing and turning thinking about the records office. Twins? Babies switched at birth? Who have similar names and traits? Finally, she threw back the covers. Who would know? The hospital? And Mrs. McDonough. Could Riley be in danger?

After a quick shower, Dorie headed back out to the *Beacon*.